SEARCH FOR THE MYSTERIOUS DRAGONFLY

AN ACTION MYSTERY NOVEL

By

ROBERT W. LINDSAY

AUTHOR'S

ACKNOWLEDGEMENTS:

Once again, my thanks and heartfelt gratitude to my wife, Mary Jean, who, without her help and encouragement, I would still be stuck, embroiled in the publishing labyrinth at LULU. Her talent at deciphering those complicated instructions allowed this work to finally be printed.

Printed in the United States of America at
www.lulu.com

First Edition

All rights reserved
Copyright by
Robert W. Lindsay, 2005

PREFACE

EAST OF MUNICH, GERMANY, MAY 1945

The dark basement in the abandoned German officer's barracks smelled of gun smoke from the battle of Berlin that was still raging only two blocks away. Obeying the officer's order, the American sergeant picked up one end of a heavy military footlocker that had been hidden under a tarp and dragged it across the mildewed basement toward the stone steps that led to the surface.

Not much older than the young sergeant, the round faced American General followed behind. Weak from the loss of blood, the officer winced with each faltering step, his bandaged hand hanging limp by his side. Gritting his teeth, he ignored the pain from the loss of three fingers on his left hand. With his mangled hand, he had still managed to crash-land his damaged plane in the midst of the raging battle. The Sergeant, ignoring his own wounds, had raced through hostile gunfire to come to the General's rescue and carried him to safety.

"Halt right there," the General said, pulling a colt 45 from his holster. The sergeant dropped the locker and turned in time to see him fire a single round into the heavy lock. The hasp fell away. In the dim light, the soldier stood back as the officer snatched at the lid with his good hand. It creaked opened and he struck a match and held it up. Tiny twinkling stars of light flickered back. Quickly, he blew out the flame. "The kraut wasn't lying," he muttered to himself. Closing the lid, he placed his own lock in the hasp and clicked it shut. "Take it to the jeep," he ordered.

The soldier obediently dragged the heavy container up a steep flight of stone steps through an opening to the vehicle parked outside the smoldering building. "That was good information he gave us at the first aid station," he said. His articulate cultured voice sounded weak, but resolute. "Lucky you were there and could interpret for me."

"Yes sir," the sergeant said, lifting the foot-locker into the jeep.

The officer rested on the jeep, swaying unsteadily on his feet. "How did you learn to speak their language so fluently?"

The wound on the sergeant's chin began to bleed again, and he deliberately touched the bandage with a probing finger. "My folks were born in Hamburg, sir. They left for America in '25."

"When we return, we must reward the kraut for such accurate information. Luckily, you understood his ravings. He was on the cot beside me, but I didn't understand a word he was saying." Cuddling his injured hand, he watched the young soldier carefully as they drove along. When the soldier noticed, the young General quickly looked down at his bandaged hand. "Doesn't seem like they're gone. I can still feel 'em."

"Yes sir," the soldier said.

The sergeant maneuvered their jeep around broken bricks from demolished buildings to a mobile field station. A Lieutenant came to the jeep and saluted. Returning the salute, the General said, "What's your name Lieutenant?"

"Abermathy, sir."

"Lieutenant Abermathy, I am General Fitzhammer."

"Yes sir. I recognize you sir."

"My driver has recently been of great service to me and to his country. I want you to enter his name on the record for a citation for bravery."

Yes sir," he said, turning to the surprised driver. "Your name and serial number, soldier."

Matthew J. Wielding, sir, serial 22446613." The Lieutenant quickly recorded the necessary information then saluted the General.

Returning the Lieutenant's salute, General Fitzhammer motioned to Sergeant Wielding to drive on. Ten minutes later, the jeep pulled through an opening that had been blown in the side of an old stone building. He drove around the corner out of sight of the road. There, a German officer lay on the floor, his hands shackled behind his back. The Sergeant got out and stood at attention.

"Wielding, when you pulled me out of my plane in the mist of battle, I was grateful. That machine-gun fire could have cut us both to ribbons."

"Yes sir," he said.

"You stayed with me at the first aid station when I was in need of extra attention. And your breviary at the plane was far beyond the call of duty. I shall always remember that."

"Thank you, sir."

Then he glanced at the prisoner and said, "We still have need of this man."

"He's almost dead, sir."

The General's blue eyes suddenly flashed angrily. "If he had not been needed, he would already be dead. Remove his uniform."

"Sir?"

"Take off his clothes, soldier. Do you not understand English?"

"Sir, the cold weather ... he needs medical attention."

"Are you disobeying my direct order?"

"No sir, but it might kill him."

"See that it doesn't. He must be alive." If the sergeant had known what was coming next, he would have refused the order. The General began to remove his own clothes. "Keep your eyes on the prisoner, soldier." Sergeant Wielding quickly finished and stood at attention, his back to the General. "This task will be completed quite soon. Then you will be free to return to our unit."

"Yes sir," he said, uncomfortable in the presence of the superior officer standing behind him completely naked.

General Fitzhammer began to put on civilian clothes that he had brought along. "Now put my uniform on him." The soldier's hands shook as he stretched the General's clothes over the motionless slightly larger body. "Now place him in the jeep." Putting the General's hat on him, Matthew realized that the German slumped in the front seat and the General appeared almost identical. Climbing into the back seat, the General said, "Now drive past the field station and on to the river."

As they drove slowly past with the canvas top up, and the two star flag flying from the jeep, the officer on duty later would swear that the general was alive and sitting in the front passenger seat.

Suddenly, as they were beside the field headquarters, an army canteen flew out and hit the sentry on duty. He turned around in time to hear a pistol shot and see the figure in the front seat slump forward.

"Keep driving, soldier," the general ordered. Through the rear mirror the young driver could see the sentry running into the tent with the canteen in his hand.

"He thinks you've been shot, sir."

"He's supposed to." As directed, Matthew stopped the jeep on a bluff high above the river. "One more job soldier. Toss that body into the water." With the General's pistol pointed at him, Sergeant Wielding dragged the body to the edge and pushed it off. The swift water quickly carried it down stream and out of sight. Ten miles farther on, Matthew loaded the footlocker onto a waiting helicopter and the General climbed on board. Turning back, he threw four diamonds at Matthew's feet. "Your reward soldier. If I were you, I'd take that jeep and get the hell out of here. The military doesn't take kindly to killing a General." The helicopter lifted off, leaving Matthew alone.

Footnote:

Sergeant Matthew Wielding did not attend his own court-martial. The evidence was overwhelming. A single diamond and a note in the General's own handwriting, found in the canteen thrown from the jeep, stated: Sergeant Wielding was caught by me with confiscated war contraband, diamonds stolen by SS soldiers from Jews in the Nazi prison camps. He has overpowered me. As I write this, I am alone for a minute. He has threatened to shoot me when he comes back, if I do not do his bidding.

The court-martial order stated: Sergeant Matthew J. Wielding, military serial 22446613, has been found guilty of murder in the first degree. He is sentenced to death by firing squad. He is still at large and considered to be extremely dangerous. Orders are to shoot on sight.

CHAPTER ONE

NORTH CAROLINA, USA 1985

Betty Ann sat up on the couch with a start. "Did you hear that Ted?" her soft feminine voice betraying her southern heritage. "There's a tornado warning over in South Carolina!"

Stripped to the waste, Ted Lowen walked into the room wiping the remainder of shaving cream from his suntanned jaw. The small half-moon shaped scar on his chin refused to relinquish the last of it, and he wiped again. In a gravelly voice that had always made her shiver with excitement, he drawled, "That's thirty miles away, Doll. It'll never reach Wingate."

Ever since he had rescued her from the water under the bridge where her little convertible had skidded into the river, she had been in love with him. She moved in that very week and never returned to the college up north. He was the father she never had and the lover she always wanted. For the last nine years she had never regretted her decision for one moment, until now.

"They've put out warnings for our area, all the way to Charlotte," she pleaded. "Must we go, Ted?"

Looking much younger than his 60 years, seldom finding the need for long sentences, he looked down at her with a steady gaze. "Got to, Doll."

The shoulder strap on her silk gown slid off one white shoulder revealing a soft round curve. "But it might come this way, Ted."

"It's important, Doll."

"But Ted, this can wait for a little while, can't it? That happened forty years ago. That was before I was even born."

He shook his head resolutely. "Get dressed." Taught muscles flexed across his chest as he ran a rough hand through his longish dark hair. "Only take thirty minutes."

"The news caster said they were searching for someone over here. He didn't mention your name."

"Changed my name," he drawled. "Said I killed a General."

"You said the general escaped to China or somewhere. They couldn't be looking for you anymore. Not after all this time."

"Gotta know for sure, Betty Ann."

"Well, if my friend is right, Mr. Walpole can search national police records any time. He'll find out after this weather gets better."

Agitated, Ted paced back and forth in the living room. "Thought I'd covered my trail."

"Don't be such a worrywart, darling," she said, walking past him into the bedroom. "With your new name, there's no way they can find you now." Through her tight shirt and dungarees, he sensed the lingering fragrance of perfumed soap on smooth skin. Coming back with a hairbrush she plopped down on the sofa, one shapely leg folded under the other, her brown eyes riveted to the TV screen. "Anyway," she said as she brushed her hair, "this storm is more important right now. I'm not leaving this set!"

He opened the door to the carport and turned back. "Take along your Walkman, Doll."

She didn't move. "Listen!" she said.

The announcer grimaced, his voice, sounding exaggerated and urgent. "A twister has been spotted near Camden, South Carolina! Viewers reported seeing trees flying through the air. Updates every hour on the hour on channel thirty-six, where you get all the news first."

Impatiently, Ted waited at the door. "Now, Betty Ann." She reluctantly turned off the TV and followed him out. A wall of gray in the eastern sky began to block out the blue. The Wingate College clock on the administration building in the next block chimed one o'clock as she entered their small foreign auto and Ted slid behind the wheel. "Gotta know what they know," he muttered.

The dark clouds seemed closer as the little Datson made its way through the college campus and turned west onto highway 74. As they passed through the small town of Wingate, Betty Ann said, "Maybe you should have picked a more remote place to live, Ted."

"It's where he lived, Doll."

"But that was a long time ago, Ted."

"He'll come back here. Said he would."

"Why are you so certain. He could go anywhere with all that wealth."

"Cause he said he would, Betty Ann."

"Maybe he just said it to throw you off. You said he had everything planned out."

"It was before we knew about the diamonds. Wasn't sure he was going to live. Dying men don't lie." They passed the tall silo at the edge of town as the Datson picked up speed. "When he does, I can prove I didn't kill him."

"That won't be the end of it, Ted."

"They'll have to drop the charges, then."

Twenty minutes later, approaching the center of Monroe, merchants were boarding up windows. Ted parked, as strong gusts began to rattle the flag on the county court house dome. The venerable old hall of justice stood guard over the many law offices surrounding it. An epitaph below the crossed sabers on a tall monolithic square stone monument out front pointing toward the rushing clouds read: "God Rest Our Confederate Soldiers."

Betty Ann got out and braced against the wind. "It's already caught up to us, Ted; I told you!"

His tall body leaned into the heavy breeze as he searched the cloud-choked sky. Hawk-like eyes stared out from under shaggy eyebrows. "Just a thunder storm."

"Well, where's the thunder then?" With the Walkman radio glued to her ear, she pointed at the low rushing clouds. "Look, they're touching the dome."

Ted saw the frown on her face. "It's only wind, Doll."

"I was in a tornado once, Ted, and I would rather not see another."

"Don't worry, Doll. I'll keep you safe."

"You better, if you know what I mean," she said, smiling grimly at his pet name for her. "You don't want your Doll to blow away, do you?" He glanced again at the sky, and picked up his pace. "Let's find this guy."

"My friend said his office is in that row of buildings," she said, pointing across the street. "Mercy Ted! The radio just said a twister touched down at Hilltop! We just came from there." She looked around fearfully, following him across the street. "I told you, Ted. That's less than five miles away!"

Ted pulled Betty Ann into an open doorway just as a trash can tumbled by. "This the place?"

"Yes," she said. They entered a long unpainted corridor. The old two-story house, converted to office space, seemed abandoned. A single raw bulb hanging from a cord at the far end of the hall lit up a grimy wall beside a stairwell. "What a dump," Betty Ann said, looking around. "His office must be upstairs." She peeked up a dimly lit rickety and narrow stairwell. Suddenly she pulled her hand away. "I' can't go into that tiny space, Ted. You know I'm claustrophobic."

"Stay here, then." She hesitated. Then squealing, she jumped ahead of him and took the stairs two at a time. Laughing, his voice reverberated in the small enclosure. "Slow down. Don't hurt yourself." When he reached the second floor, Betty Ann was waiting beside a partly opened door in a hallway. The frosted glass window in its center had with several names partially scratched off. It now simply read, Walpole.

She whispered, "This is it, Ted."

He pushed the door and it swung open. He stepped into an unlit room, Betty Ann followed close behind him. The odor of kerosene and musty fabric mixed with cigar smoke hung in the air. "Hello," he called out.

"There's no one here, Ted," she whispered. Two metal folding funeral chairs, were placed facing each other around a rickety card table. A lamp without a bulb, its paisley shade tilted at a roguish angle sat in the middle of the dark room. Betty Ann wrinkled her nose. "What's that smell?"

Ted shrugged and turned to leave, then hesitated when a phone somewhere began to ring. Behind a partially closed door beyond the table, a light came on in an adjoining room. A sliver of silver light splashed across a rough wood floor and onto part of the opposite wall. In large letters someone had drawn with their finger on the dusty partition: *SUPPORT MENTAL HEALTH – OR I'LL KILL YOU.*

They listened as a voice in the other room whined, "Wait a minute, will ya? Let me write it down." After a moment of silence, the voice spoke again. "Yeah, sure. Well don't worry about it."

Suddenly, something moved in the dark corner beyond the light. Poking Ted, Betty Ann whispered, "Over there ... look!"

Ted bristled as a figure stepped into the light. "I'm sorry if I startled you," the young man said timidly. He was shorter than Ted by several inches with shaggy black hair.

Not more than eighteen, Betty Ann thought.

"I must have fallen asleep." The rumpled jeans and black T-shirt that he wore looked slept in. "I think he'll be off the phone soon. He's had me waiting out here for a while."

"You a client?" Ted asked.

"Well ... yes; guess you're wondering why I was here in the dark."

Ted shrugged.

Betty Ann relaxed and eased around from behind Ted. He had a trusting face, devoid of guile. His brown eyes peered out from behind big round glasses that clung to a button nose.

She held out her hand. "My name is Betty Ann and this is Ted." As he reached for it, she caught the pleasing aroma of his after-shave.

"My name's Mark Lindsay. I know this sounds silly, but I was sitting in the dark and fell asleep." Betty Ann took his outstretched hand and grinned. "Do you always sleep in offices?"

He smiled weakly. "Well, I haven't been getting much lately," he grinned sheepishly, "sleep, that is." Absentmindedly scratching his arm, he continued, "You see I'm supposed to keep a low profile."

"Well, bless your heart," Betty Ann said glancing at Ted. "How long have you been doing it ... you know, keeping a low profile?"

"Just two days, but it seems like forever. This is the last place they would look for me." He scratched his arm again. "Anyway, I'm waiting for him to set things up."

Suddenly the light spilling on the floor went out. Ted walked across the darkened room and stuck his head through the partially open door. The man sitting in a large overstuffed office chair, with his back turned, faced an open window. His head barely showed above the backrest. He wore a business suit and a dark snap-brim hat pushed far back on his head. He was mumbling into a phone pressed to his left ear while his other hand made wild gestures in the air.

From the doorway, Ted said gruffly, "You getting off that phone soon?"

The little man swung the chair around, eyes wide with terror. He said in a strained nasal whine, "Who the hell are you?" At the same time his hand reached into an open desk drawer. Before Ted could reply, the hand came out holding a silver plated revolver. Carefully, he pointed it at Ted. "I said, who the frigging hell *are* you?"

Suddenly, the building began to shake and Betty Ann rushed into the room. "Tornado!" she screamed.

The little man lowered his weapon, and slammed the phone down without saying goodbye. Ignoring the hysterical woman he said, "Is she wit' you? Hell ... I thought you was one of dem!"

"You Walpole?" Ted asked, one eye on the gun.

His prominent Brooklyn accent grating on their nerves, he whined, "Who wants-ta know?" Suddenly an airborne tree limb hit the building and the old house shook under the impact.

"Look at that!" Ted said, pointing outside. It had grown very dark.

Walpole's eyes focused on the window. Distracted by the storm, he mumbled, "Doze guys would walk true hell to get me if day knew what I know."

"Doll, you might be right!" Ted muttered.

"Who the hell *are* you?" Walpole said, swinging back around, aware of him again.

At that moment Mark walked in. "Have you made any progress, Mr. Walpole. I can't wait much longer."

Without warning, a sound, like a freight train, drowned out his words. Holes suddenly materialized in the wall behind Ted's head. Haratio Morgan Walpole quickly rose from his swivel chair and bolted for the door. He was fast for such a small man. "Dat's not no train! And dis ain't no bomb shelter," he yelled as he ran through the doorway and headed for the stairwell.

Mark snatched an object from the desk and put it in his shirt pocket. "This is mine," he said defensively when he saw Betty Ann's reproachful expression.

Grabbing her hand, Ted followed close on Walpole's heels, the chilling sound of wood tearing suddenly all around them. As they entered the stairwell the raw light bulb flickered and went out. The old structure shook and heeled over several degrees. They groped for handholds along an unfamiliar slanting wall in the pitch-black staircase. Nothing seemed to be where it was supposed to be. Desperately, Mark pushed Betty Ann and Ted ahead of him.

The roar outside intensified and the structure moved again under their feet. The two following behind Ted piled up against him on the slanted steps. Betty Ann squealed struggling to untangle herself from arms and legs. "What happened, Ted?"

"It's Walpole ... I think." He put his hand behind the still form on the floor and felt a barrier that had not been there before. "He's out cold. ran into a wall."

Betty Ann pulled at Ted's arm. "Ted, get us out, get us out, get us out!"

"I'm trying!" He felt around the small space; the barrier seemed solid. "Not this way. Have to go back."

Mark yelled above the noise, "We can't. Steps missing at the top. I know, I tried." Screeching tearing sounds of rupturing timbers filled the air and the old building suddenly rolled farther over on its edge.

Betty Ann covered her ears, her heart pounded furiously, she pleaded, "Please Ted, I don't want to die."

Pushing Walpole aside, he frantically pulled at jagged broken boards. "Damned thing's blocked!" Up the stairwell where the roof had once been, racing clouds now rushed by. Once attached to the roof, one by one, top edges of the ragged wall began to give way.

Now, dim light filtered down through the dust-clogged cavity and they could see again. "Look out!" Mark yelled, as part of the structure up above broke loose and fell. The heavy object skipping down the staircase, plowing a deep groove as it narrowly missed them. Wedged in the stairwell, it swayed precariously close. Another beam above their heads began to flex, threatening to break loose.

Mark, pointing to a jagged hole that had not been there seconds before, "Behind you!"

Ted felt fresh air pouring through near the floor. "Last one ripped a hole." Poking his head and arm through the opening, he pushed at a heavy object on the other side blocking his way. It moved a couple of inches then refused to go farther! "Hurry Mark, help me!" Quickly they pushed at a heavy cabinet partially blocking the jagged hole. It didn't budge.

Ted pulled Betty Ann to the hole. "Big enough for you, Doll. Hurry!" Quickly, she slipped through and fell to the floor in the hallway.

She pleaded, "Try to squeeze through, Ted. You've got to!"

"Too small; save yourself."

Debris rained down as Betty Ann searched for some object in the hallway that could be use as a lever to move the heavy cabinet blocking the hole. There was nothing. Again, the building shook violently and like a spent arrow returning from the sky, a beam fell through near the front door.

Ted yelled. "Get out, it's all coming down!" Glass exploded inward toward her and suddenly fear overpowered her determination to help. Feeling her way through the thick cloud of dust, she found the door.

Stepping outside, gulping in the cleaner air, she noticed the fallen crossbeam. Quickly, running back into the swaying building, she dragged the long 4 by 4 behind her. "Use this," she yelled. Placing one end into a crack in the floor beside her, she said, "like a lever." Together the two men forced the heavy piece of furniture to the side, and pulled Mr. Walpole out into the hallway. Behind them in the stairwell, a second heavy wall fell, filling the shaft with more dust and debris. Then, unexpectedly, the roaring train noise stopped.

CHAPTER TWO

Together Mark and Ted pulled Mr. Walpole's limp body to the entrance and sat him on the sidewalk, his back against the wall. Rain began to fall. Suddenly, Walpole's eyes popped open. Groaning, he grabbed his hip. "What happened?"

Betty Ann rolled her jacket up for a pillow and placed it under his head. "Bless your heart, Mr. Walpole. You've been in a tornado."

"Don't remember a damned ting after da lights went out. What'd I miss?"

"Well, for one thing, your old building collapsed."

Distractedly, he felt his hip. "Dat ain't my building."

Mark took his arm. "Can you stand?"

Walpole winced. "Leave me alone, can't-cha? My hip ain't right."

The deserted street began to fill with people. Betty Ann looked around at the broken buildings and shredded trees. "Well, at least the courthouse made it." Coming toward them, an Emergency Van maneuvered around the debris in the street and pulled up across the street. Betty Ann watched as men in white coats ran into a crumpled structure.

She said, "Looks like someone's hurt over there."

"Over here too," Walpole whined, trying to get to his feet. Help me over to dat meat wagon, will ya? My hip still ain't right." Together, they assisted him to the rescue vehicle just as two white-coated men came back out.

"It'll take a wrecking crane to get him out," one said talking to someone on the other end of a radiophone. "He was dead the second that wall hit him. Police will want to ask questions about that rifle he had. It had a silencer on it."

Suddenly, the white coats spotted Walpole leaning against the Van. "You need some help, sir?"

"Sheesh, can't you yahoos figure dat out?" They put him on a gurney and shoved him inside. "Watch-it, can't-cha! I'm hurting real bad here." As the ambulance pulled away, they could hear him yelling, "Dat hurts, damn-it! Don't touch me no more!"

"What a fowl mouth," Betty Ann said. "What's a silencer, Ted?"

Ted looked grimly at Mark, who looked away, avoiding eye contact. "Keeps the sound down."

"Why would they need it?"

Ted avoided her eyes and mumbled, "To shoot someone. I guess."

Mark rolled his eyes at Betty Ann. "That silencer is the second weird thing that's happened to me. Someone tried to kidnap me earlier"

"Bless your heart, Mark, are you rich? Were they after a ransom?"

"How many rich people do you know that live in a trailer park?" He grinned sheepishly. "I can hardly pay my rent."

"Could they have mistaken you for someone else?" Not waiting for an answer, she gazed up and down the street. "Wonder if Matilda made it? She was just around the corner."

"You left some woman out in the street!"

With an impish grin, Betty Ann took Mark's hand and led him along the sidewalk, while Ted followed behind them. "Come on, I'll introduce you to her."

"You mean if she's still alive, don't you?"

"Don't worry about Matilda; she's ridden out much worse. Before Ted found her, she'd just been through a hurricane at the beach."

"Outside?"

"Uh-huh, hidden behind an all night Laundromat." As they dodged a downed telephone wire and turned the corner Betty Ann exclaimed, "There she is." She patted the hood of a small rusty foreign automobile. "Mark, meet Matilda. Looks like her rust kept her glued together again."

Mark looked relieved. "This is Matilda?"

Grinning, Betty Ann climbed into the passenger side of the little Datson and turned on the car radio. Through the open door, Ted and Mark listened to the broadcast. A somber voice was warning the radio audience, urging all to find shelter. Another twister cloud had been spotted in the area."

Ted came around and got behind the wheel. "Wonder if the house in Wingate is still there?"

Betty Ann grinned at Mark. "I sure hope your car made it through as well as Matilda. We'll be more than happy to drive you to where it's parked."

"Oh, it's not far," Mark said, "I can walk."

"Heavens no. We can't let you do that." Holding her hand out she wiggled her fingers and inviting him into the vehicle. "You can sit on my lap; the back seat is full of junk."

Hesitantly, Mark sat down. "It's in the next block," he said, pointing a thumb over his shoulder. Ted wheeled Matilda around in the street and began to maneuver past a fallen telephone pole while Betty Ann leaned around Mark and twirled the radio dial.

Abruptly, music was interrupted by a tense voice. "A funnel cloud touched down in the Union County town of Monroe. The twister wrecked a total of five buildings. Then it touched down again near the K-mart shopping center west of town, cutting a quarter-mile swath all the way to Sweet Union Flea Market. An alert is still in effect."

Mark peered grimly through the windshield. "It was parked right in here." A large downed oak tree completely blocked the avenue; its branches tangled in sparking wires. With each arc, resembling Strobes at a Go-Go club, glaring blue light flashed through the limbs. "There it is!" Mark said, "under that tree!"

"And mashed flat!" Betty Ann said, shaking her head sadly. "Bless your heart, Mark. It will never work again!"

"Guess I'll have to take a taxi to Sweet Union."

"Is that where your little house is?" Betty Ann said sadly. Then her face lit up. "I have a wonderful idea, Mark! If it's all right with Ted, why don't you come home with us? That trailer park was right in the path of that old twister." He glanced at Ted who shrugged his shoulders and nodded.

Considering the invitation, Mark stared at the live wires sparking in the old tree. Suddenly he looked relieved and grinned sheepishly. "When I heard that radio announcer say where the storm hit, I was wondering what I was gonna do."

Settling back on Betty Ann's lap, he watched the road as Ted drove Matilda away from downtown. Crossing over a bridge spanning railroad tracks, they traveled down Skyway Drive and turned eastward onto highway 74. As the road became clearer, Ted picked up speed.

Passing the hospital across from Bo Jangles Restaurant, Betty Ann exclaimed, "Look at all the ambulances! Must be ten or twelve, all unloading at the same time."

"Wonder how Mr. Walpole's doing?" Mark said, grimily, "He was all I could afford ... and my only hope."

Betty Ann glanced at Ted. "You're too young to be down to your last hope, Mark. After you get some hot food in your stomach, you'll feel better."

"Sounds good, Betty Ann, but it won't help my problem."

"What on earth do you mean, Mark?"

"I'd rather not say. You probably wouldn't believe me if I told you."

CHAPTER THREE

Ted pulled Matilda into the gas station at the top of the hill where the radio had said the twister had touched down. Miraculously, the pumps still worked. Ted began to pump gas. Mark removed himself from Betty Ann's lap and stretched his legs. She wrinkled her nose, an inquisitive look on her face and asked through the open door, "Why were you in Mr. Walpole's office, Mark?"

"Got his name out of the phone book."

"You're so young. Why on earth would you need a private detective?"

He looked away.

"Come on Mark. We're your friends now. You can tell me."

Mark hesitated for a minute before he spoke. Betty Ann thought he was going to cry. Suddenly words began to tumble out. "I'd been working on a computer program using a new logic. Several codes became scrambled and somehow it caused something extraordinary to happen." His eyes filled with apprehension. "The thing breaks security codes. Cuts through them like a hot knife through butter."

"What does that mean?"

"It can break passwords, Betty Ann," he said.

Ted grinned as he stepped back into Matilda. "Programmers been doing that for years."

Mark sat back on Betty Ann's lap and closed the door. "But this works really fast, Ted! Broke an account in less than a minute. Shortest time I ever heard of was four hours." He looked off into the distance, an uncomfortable expression on his young face. Then he continued. "Tested it on a company called Corsair Enterprises. Got through two password firewalls in less than a minute."

Ted turned the idea over in his mind. "You could become rich."

"Yeah, or dead maybe."

Betty Ann looked shocked. "Dead! Who would want to kill you?"

"Somebody at Corsair Enterprises. That's what I'm trying to tell you. I found over twenty different passwords inside that one database."

"But how could Mr. Walpole help you, Mark?"

"I'm getting to that, Betty Ann. Once I started breaking into 'em, I couldn't stop myself. It was like eating peanuts. I was in and out in less than fifteen minutes. Don't know for sure, but I think they must deal in illegal money."

"Payoffs?"

Mark nodded, looking frightened. "Every time I broke into an account, a set of figures would pop up. Maybe a money laundering thing."

"Oh mercy! You suppose they're gangsters?"

"There were transactions totaling hundreds of thousands of dollars. All in numbered accounts with a crazy scribbling across the top - strange hieroglyphics, some sort of secret language."

Betty Ann glanced at Ted, "Have you told anyone else about this, Mark?"

"Only Mr. Walpole, about breaking the password codes, but he didn't seem interested." Mark looked uncomfortable. "There is one other person that knows part of it. Before I tested it, I talked to a buddy on the Internet in a private chat room. His e-mail name is Dragonfly; mine is Buttercup. I swore him to secrecy, but he put a notice on a bulletin board, anyway. It said that Buttercup was bragging that he might have found a quick way to break password protections. I think he was jealous. He doesn't know my real name, though."

"What about Corsair Enterprises?" Betty Ann ask, "Can they find you?"

"I'm not sure, but they had a program of their own. It traced me back to the Computer House USA phone bank where I had logged on." He smiled grimly. "Most of us employees go on line every day."

"Then they can't find you?"

"Think they have." Mark stared at Betty Ann, his eyes big and frightened. "Since then I've had several messages on my answering machine at home. They sounded strange and there have been weird hits on my e-mail. I shut down my computer and after that last message, I even disconnected the telephone at the trailer."

"My goodness, Mark. What was the message?"

He suddenly looked older. "It appeared on my FAX machine first, only six hours after I bragged to Dragonfly. It said, we know who you are. Do not divulge what you have found ... or delete, delete, delete."

"Mercy, what does that mean?"

"I can guess, Betty Ann. But I can't bring myself to say it out loud. They sent the same message to every employee at Computer House USA. Those guys think it's a joke, but I know better."

"Did it come from the company you broke into?"

"Don't know. Somehow, they managed to erase their return address. Tried to look up Corsair Enterprises in the phone book. They're not listed, so I can't mail it back to 'em."

"Oh my, what will you do now?"

"Wish I'd never stumbled across it. Mr. Walpole was supposed to help me give the disk back."

"Take it to the IRS."

"Yes, Mark, Ted's right," Betty Ann said, "You could get a reward. They pay a percentage of what they catch."

"You have proof?" Ted asked. "You need evidence."

"Oh, I have proof all right." Mark held up a little round plastic disk. "I downloaded everything onto this."
Looking frightened, he continued, "and now they know I've got it."

A few minutes after passing a tall grain elevator with restless pigeons flying around the top, they pulled up to a stoplight. Mark asked, "This Wingate?"

"Oh my goodness yes, Mark," Betty Ann cooed. "This is our little village." Past the traffic light, Ted turned Matilda left through a large stone gate. They crossed over railroad tracks and through the Wingate College campus. Maintenance men guided oversized lawn mowers across putting green quality grass. Students hurried back and forth. In the setting sun, dormitory buildings cast long cool shadows across lush expanses. "We're almost home," Betty Ann said proudly.

A block later, Ted maneuvered Matilda onto a wide driveway and came to a stop in a double sized carport.

"You almost live on campus, Ted!"

"Pretty close."

Mark looked past two giant Water Oaks on the front lawn and noticed a turquoise colored house across the street. "What an odd color."

"Isn't it," Betty Ann chuckled. "For a while the postman put our mail in their box, because the number six on their street number became loose and hung upside down. Looked like a nine to him, and that's our number." Mark followed them past a porch swing on the long open front porch to the front door. Stepping into their large living room, Mark said, "This sure beats my trailer."

Ted turned on the TV. "Time for news," he said as it lit up. Scenes of destruction filled the screen. Rescue workers were removing the man killed when the building collapsed. People were standing behind a yellow police tape, gawking.

Immediately, Mark noticed a long black limousine parked beside a phone booth. A man, standing with the door open, was talking on the phone. "Hey! That's the guy that tried to pull me into the limo this morning."

Ted leaned closer to the screen. "You sure?"

"Recognized the car first; it stopped right beside me. They almost dragged me into the back seat." Betty Ann came over and studied the scene closely as Mark continued. "If a police car hadn't shown up, he would of too. When the cops turned in our direction, the limo took off like a bat out of hell."

"They didn't go after it?"

"No," he said grimly. "Instead they stopped and questioned me, like I was a criminal! Asked me if I'd been trying to rob the man."

"Oh, Mark, why didn't you explain that to them? They would have understood."

"It would have been my word against his, and with all the money he must have had for high priced lawyers and all, I wouldn't have stood a chance." For the first time she understood how vulnerable he felt. "Would you have believed me?"

"Oh my, yes. You're a nice clean-cut boy. And you don't look at all like a mugger to me."

They watched as the man in the dark suit got into the car and it drove away. "Can you make out that license number, Betty Ann?"

"It's covered up! Looks like a Jersey plate though."

"Shiny washed car." Ted's eyebrows knitted. "Mud on the tag?"

Mark frowned. "Looks like they didn't want anyone reading their tag number."

"Well, you're safe now, Mark," Betty Ann said. "Are you hungry?" Without waiting for an answer she went into the kitchen. "I'll fix us all a light repast."

After peanut butter and jelly sandwiches, Mark stood up. "This has been great. Now, if I can just get somebody to drive me to the trailer park. I need some of my stuff." Mark caught the exasperated look Ted gave Betty Ann and said quickly, "If everything's still okay there, I'll be out of your hair for good."

"Oh Mark, must you go?" Betty Ann pleaded.

"Think so. My little trailer is waiting."

"In that case, Ted will be glad to drive you over there." She stood up defiantly looking back at Ted. "And I'll come along too." They crowded into the little car, this time Betty Ann sat on Mark's lap.

At Sweet Union Flea Market, that had once been an outdoor movie theater, everything was a mess. Tables were overturned and the tornado had scattered debris in every direction.

"Now where, Mark?"

"My trailer is over that rise." He pointed at a hill on the other side of a wire fence. Not far off, a rustic lane led in a long curve over the hill. Tree limbs were strewn across it, blocking the way.

"We can't get through that way, Mark."

"That's okay, Betty Ann; I'll walk from here."

"What if something has happened to your little home, Mark? You'll be stranded out here all alone."

"I can manage."

"At least let Ted get you closer." Driving over the dirt mounds placed there so that the cars would be elevated for a better view of the movie screen he brought Matilda to a stop at the fence at the far end. "We'll wait here for you, Mark. If your trailer is okay, come back to the top of that hill and wave."

"Thanks, Betty Ann" Mark said, as he started to open the door. Suddenly, Betty Ann grabbed his hand.

"Wait. Don't get out! A car just pulled in on the road over yonder!" She hastily pushed Mark's head down below the window level. "I saw it in the side mirror."

"Where?"

"Keep down, Mark. It's by that old fallen tree, close to the highway." She adjusted the mirror for a better view. "It's the same limo we saw on TV!"

The man in the expensive suit got out and swiftly walked past the fallen tree and up to the top of the hill a quarter of a mile away. He stood very still staring off into the distance.

"Ted, he's watching Mark's trailer!" In spite of himself, Mark poked his head up.

"That's him all right!"

"Oh Mark, they *do* know where you live!"

"But they don't know this car," Ted growled, starting the motor. Speeding back across the uneven mounds of earth, Matilda raced toward the exit, engine whining each time her wheels cleared an uneven mound.

The man in black, turn and held something up to his face. "Oh My goodness, he has binoculars! Mark, stay down." Ted guided Matilda onto highway 74 as the figure followed their progress. Again, Mark poked his head up. "I told you to keep down, Mark," Betty Ann said, pushing him back down.

Suddenly, the man pulled a pistol from a should-holster and fired. The bullet thumped into the car, and Ted shoved the gas-pedal to the floor. As Matilda picked up speed, a second shot rang ricocheting across the roof. Then the gunman broke into a trot, running toward his parked automobile.

Ted kept the pedal pressed to the floor all the way back to Monroe. Dodging in and out of traffic, he ran the red light at Wal-mart's shopping center. At Quincy's, the traffic was stopped for a fender bender. A cop was slowly directing all traffic onto a side street.

"What can we do, Ted? He'll catch us!"

Ted pulled into the turning lane as close as he dared behind a waiting heavily loaded flat bed truck. "Take this back road."

"He must have seen Mark!" She scanned the highway behind them. "He wants you bad, Mark."

Precious seconds went by before the policeman waved them on. As Ted followed the turning truck onto the two-lane road, he glanced in his rearview mirror one last time. There, a half-mile back, he saw the black limo just coming into view. "Damn! He saw us turn."

Halfway up the crest of a long hill, Ted jumped around the slow moving flat bed and whipped back in just in time to miss an eighteen-wheeler cresting the rise. In his rearview mirror he could see the hood of the pursuing automobile waiting for his chance to turn. "Good, There's traffic between us."

A mile back, the policeman waved the black car on. Driving on the wrong side of the road, it whipped around three cars and ducked back into the right lane narrowly avoiding a collision. Then it jumped into the on coming lane again, passing two more before quickly swerving back.

Horrified, Mark watched over his shoulder. "Still back there, Ted!"

At a warning light Ted made a hard right, racing through a neighborhood of small homes. Two blocks later, a stoplight turned red. "Hold on ... gonna be dicey." He jumped the light going flat out. A car coming from their left slammed on breaks just missing them.

Betty Ann looked through the back window. "He's going to catch us, Ted!"

"There's another road," Ted said through gritted teeth. "Look for it."

"Down yonder, Ted," Betty Ann pointed at a spot a hundred yards ahead. He took the street on two wheels, fishtailing in the loose dirt then he guided Matilda along the twisting lane.

Mark spoke up. "I saw him cresting the hill back there just as you turned. He's coming fast!"

In front of them, the unpaved road curved sharply at the base of a steep hill. There it crossed a highway. Ted slammed on the breaks and then wheeled Matilda onto the hard surface. Suddenly he realized where he was. Two quick turns, one to the left and another to the right, and he pulled Matilda into their driveway and around behind the house. "Cross your fingers," he said.

Entering the house through the back door, Betty Ann rushed to a front window and looked out through gauze-thin drapes. The road was empty. "Mercy, that was too close," she said. Then the black limo crested the distant rise coming very fast. "It's on Camden Road!" she shrieked. "What can we do?"

CHAPTER FOUR

From behind the drapes, they watched in the darkened room as the stretch limo suddenly slowed down to a crawl. "Oh my goodness!" Betty Ann said, holding tight to Ted's arm. "They're like blood hounds! What can we do?"

Mark reached for a phone. "I'll call the police. Let them handle it."

Ted grabbed his hand. "Don't. What cops know … they'll soon know."

"I'll have to take that chance, Ted. Not worth it … putting you two in danger."

"We're in it now," he said, glancing darkly at Betty Ann. "No cops."

Suddenly the limo came to a stop and a patrol car they hadn't noticed before pulled up beside it. Betty Ann started for the door. "I'm going to tell." Ted grabbed her arm and shook his head. They watched from behind the curtains, as the two drivers spoke to each for several seconds, then the limo continued moving up Camden Road. The cruiser followed close behind, driving slowly past the house. "Whose side is he on, Ted?"

"Cruiser's not local. No door emblem."

Betty Ann's eyes opened wide. "They're together!"

Pulling a small disk from his pocket, Mark said, "Do you have a computer?"

"It's in the back room, Mark," Betty Ann said, watching the road from the window. "I'm going to stay right here … in case they come back."

In the back room, with Ted looking over his shoulder, Mark placed the shinny device into a drive slot and a few keystrokes later entered a screen that Ted had never seen before. "How'd you do that?"

"Went through DOS. It's an invisible operating system behind the Windows program. Normally, you'd never know it's there." Ted watched as he checked to make sure there was enough disk space. Then he downloaded everything off the floppy. "It'll be on your hard drive in a minute."

"You make it look easy."

Mark grinned. "We need a password."

"How about Mark spelled backwards?" Ted offered, chuckling to himself.

"KRAM! That'll work. And it's something we can remember."

The first file to appear had a combination of odd symbols across the top.

"This is what I was telling you about, Ted!" Below the string of symbols there were five columns, one with dates, one with single letters of the alphabet and the other three contained numbers.

"Have you ever seen anything like that before?"

Ted shook his head. "Let's see another one." The next file was similar except for the arrangement of numbers. "It's a code of some kind."

"They never came back," Betty Ann said, as she entered the computer room. "And that doesn't hurt my feelings one little bit." Standing behind Mark, she stared into the glowing screen. "What are all those little squiggles?"

"That's what we're trying to find out right now." He brought up another entry.

Scrolling down the list of accounts, they saw that each one had the same series of mystifying arrows and triangles, followed by rows of figures. "Someone went to a lot of trouble designing this stuff," Mark said. "I'll e-mail some of this to my internet buddy. If anyone can figure it out, Dragonfly can." Leaving out the figures, he copied the strange hieroglyphics and sent them on along with a note.

"While he's at it, maybe he can find out about Corsair Enterprises."

"I've already tried that, Betty Ann. I can't find it listed anywhere."

Betty Ann glanced at a clock on the wall. "Look at the time. That little bitty old sandwich just didn't hold me. I'm starved to death." Ted, engrossed in watching Mark typing the e-mail, said nothing. When she got no response, she continued, "The special at the Klondike today is fried chicken. Do you like fried chicken, Mark?"

"Doesn't everybody," he said, standing up. "The treat's on me."

With Mark's help, Ted removed the junk in the back seat and piled it in the back yard. Minutes later, Ted parked Matilda on a dirt parking lot behind the local eatery. The ancient one story brick building located on the corner of highway 74 and Main Street was nestled close beside the town's only stoplight. Behind the restaurant a railroad track, running parallel to the highway, separated it from the several other businesses in the college community.

While Ted stayed behind to lock the car, Betty Ann led Mark through a side door. Chimes on the college tower a block away finished striking six as they entered. The setting sun, shinning through the open door, lit up ancient grease-stained stucco walls. Mark followed her, under the high roofed ceiling fans turning lazily, past booths with checkerboard tablecloths, and on past a long counter with round barstools resting on a frayed linoleum floor.

"Boy, this place is old," Mark whispered.

"They have a reputation for the best hamburgers in the county," she said. "Traveling salesmen come way out of their way just to eat here." Beside a large picture window, they slipped into a booth with sagging imitation leather vinyl seats. Betty Ann cooed, "Wait 'till you taste the food. You'll love it."

Mark eased away from an offending seat spring that poked at him. "For certain, they don't come for the view." He stared incredulously at a narrow sidewalk outside the window only inches from the busy highway. "That road is too close, Betty Ann."

"Yes. When I used to visit my aunt here, the road was way over yonder," she said, pointing to the middle of the four-lane thoroughfare. "Then they widened it."

The stoplight outside turned red and Mark listened to the sound of whining tires as the traffic slowed to a stop. "Well, it's too close now."

Just then, Ted walked up looking unsettled. "You're sitting in a window seat, Betty Ann!"

"Of course we are, Ted. This is by far the best seat in the room."

"It's just fine with me," Mark said, grinning. "I like the view."

Betty Ann noticed Ted's jaw muscles working. "What's wrong?"

"Our limo's back!"

"Oh mercy, Ted, they're still in the neighborhood?"

"Passed by a minute ago."

"Did they see us?"

"Don't think so."

"They may come back, Ted! We should move."

"Unless you enjoy taking chances?" he said, sarcastically, leading them to a table farther from the window.

A blush began to spread down Betty Ann's neck. As she leaned over to sit down across from him, he tried unsuccessfully to pull his eyes away. The delightful view that her low cut blouse revealed, pink skin turning pinker, attracted him like a moth to a flame. Their eyes met and his ears turned red. Giggling, she leaned over toward Ted and whispered, "Sorry honey. I should have known better than to sit in the window seat."

Outside, the light turned to green and traffic resumed as a waitress delivered a folded menu with a sketch of the building on its front. Across the top in bold black letters were the words: "*THE KLONDIKE.*" Inside, crudely hand printed, were three choices of hamburger sandwiches to choose from along with the chicken special.

After finishing his meal, Mark strolled over to an ice-cream box beside the counter. He looked in for a moment then turned back toward the table. "How about some desert?" Absorbed in a heated conversation in whispered tones, Ted and Betty Ann didn't hear him. Mark glanced through the window at the fading sky, and turned back toward the ice-cream box.

Suddenly the door behind him opened. Mark turned in time to see a tall thin man enter the room. He wore an odd looking soft velvet cap with a foot long purple plume attached to it. His trousers were of the same dark material and his white shirt was decorated with lacy cuffs.

He stood very still, his chin jutting out defiantly, only his eyes moved. They darted inquisitively around the restaurant confronting each face for a second, then moving on to the next. Suddenly his dark eyes fell on Mark. "Good day young sir." Mark, instantly on guard, shifted tensely from one foot to the other. "I do believe I shall never become acclimated to this extreme weather," he said, in a stage voice heard all the way to the other end of the room. "Does not this summer seem the fouler for it?"

Mark relaxed and glanced at Ted, whose attention was still absorbed in the conversation with Betty Ann. "I guess so." He said cautiously.

"Allow me to introduce myself, young sir. Me moniker is Alexius Wickersham, late of the Shakespearean theater of London, England. Mayhap you have heard of me?" Mark shook his head. "Aye, it was ever thus." He removed the cap and bowed to his new audience. "Could I but have a moment of your time? Then away I be."

His face, with soft pallid skin and deep-set eyes framed by scraggly gray hair held Mark's attention in a firm grip. "Sure, I guess so," Mark stammered.

Running slender translucent fingers through his thinning hair his lips formed a thin frown. "This bistro rivals days glare at noon. Let us to that darker booth partake."

Mark nodded, and still cautious but now quite curious, followed him past Ted and Betty Ann, to the next booth. He sat down across from him. "How can I help you, sir?"

"Me thinks, to straightforward be is much a better scheme. Succinctly put, some devilish varlet has, with ignoble malice, forced my conveyance into a moat."

"Your car's in a ditch somewhere?"

"Alas, with bonnet bent and engine spent."

"And you need someone to pull it out?"

"Oh, that it were only so, young sir. I'm afraid said transportation is beyond repair."

"That bad? What happened?"

"Done in by a long black chariot. Not stopping, even to appraise their dastardly deed."

Mark blurted out, much louder than he expected to, "Was it a black limousine with tinted windows and New Jersey plates?"

"I know not of plates, nor cutlery. Panes of glass, dark as a witch's heart, they were … no doubt protecting from my view, Lucifer's wretched kinsman concealed within."

"The devil, you say!" Betty Ann said, turning around toward them overhearing their conversation. "That must be the same one that chased us earlier!"

"Rapscallions all, I proclaim. Coincidence this is not. Share we a common fate?" The old man stood and turned toward Betty Ann.

Mark said quickly, "Betty Ann. Let me introduce you to Mr. Alexius Wickersham, a new acquaintance of mine. Mr. Wickersham, this is Betty Ann."

Eyebrows high, glancing back at Mark for a second as he took her out stretched hand and lightly touched it to his lips. "What angel wakes me from such deep despair? A vision lovely to behold, we share."

Betty Ann withdrew her hand and smiled quizzically at Mark. "You are a poet, Mr. Wickersham?"

"Nay fair lady, only parroting do I dispense coined paraphrases from the immortal Avon prince."

Mark said, beaming proudly, "Ted, this is Mr. Wickersham. He's here all the way from England."

The old gentleman offered a limp hand to Ted. Ted shook it suspiciously. "What brings you here?"

"Holiday first … now vengeance does more appeal my appetite."

Mark butted in. "He was forced off the road by a long black limo, Ted, with tinted windows!"

"Oh?" Ted shot a warning glance at Mark, then he smiled guardedly. "Don't believe I've ever met an Englishman up close before."

"Fear not. If you prick us, do we not bleed the same as you?"

Ted smiled, concealing his amusement, he said, "If you say so."

Betty Ann broke into the conversation. "Do you have relatives here, Mr. Wickersham?"

"Nay, once there was a child, but never more."

"What happened?"

"I could not say." He hung his head. "Few love to hear the sins they loved to act. So said Pericles, scene 1."

Betty Ann knitted her eyebrows. "So you're here on vacation?"

Ted glared at her, a warning tone in his voice," He's moving on soon, Betty Ann."

She scowled back at him defiantly. "He can't leave without his car, Ted."

Wickersham glanced at Ted then his piercing eyes came back to rest on Betty Ann. "Aye, with transport in disrepair, moving on is no option fare."

"You poor poor man. You have no way to leave?" Betty Ann said, mother's instinct taking over. "I'll bet you haven't eaten all day! You do look famished."

"Oh, fair lady, not since Chaucer's calling cock spake last; and roused me from a fitful sleep, without repast."

"You haven't had any supper? You poor man." Betty Ann motioned to a waitress and whispered instructions in her ear. Soon she returned with a large poppy-seed bun with hamburger meat filled to overflowing, hash-brown potatoes and a tall glass of iced tea. "After you eat this, things will seem less grim."

His long face became more melancholy as he gazed at the food before him. "What delicious morsels and aroma fine. Without a purse," his soulful eyes fixed back onto Betty Ann again, and he said, "I surly must decline."

"If you mean you can't pay for it, don't worry. This is on us," she said, pushing the plate toward him.

Grateful eyes looked up into hers. "At that retched ditch, dame consciousness partially withdrew, then altogether fled. On waking from my ordeal grim, I scaled brambles to the lane above and found meager transportation here. Alas ... then did I discover ... I had no cash." First he nibbled at an edge, then took a large bite. His eyes grew large with delight. "'Tis an ill cook that licks not his own fingers. I'll wager this one has a happy tongue."

Protective as a mother hen, Betty Ann covered his hand with hers. "Where will you sleep tonight?"

Before answering he hesitated, meticulously cleaned every scrap from his plate. Then he looked into her eyes, an expression of regret on his face. "The air is warm, the sky is clear, my crib will be a thicket near."

"My goodness, what does that mean?"

"Betty Ann," Mark said, "he said he's going to sleep on the ground."

Betty Ann bristled. "NO WAY! You're coming home with us. You're not going to sleep outside, if I have anything to say about it." Ignoring Ted's uneasy frown, she smiled sweetly. "You'll find that southern hospitality is still alive and thriving in our little town."

It was dark when Ted pulled Matilda into the driveway. Mr. Wickersham got out, turned and smiled, giving Betty Ann his outstretched fingers to hold while she exited the car. She blushed. "Why thank you sir. You make me feel like a lady and I dearly love it."

Touching his lips to her hand before returning it, in a brooding stage voice he said, "Love is a smoke made with the fume of sighs, being purged, a fire sparkling in lovers' eyes, being vexed, a sea nourished with lovers' tears. What is it else? A madness most discreet, a choking gall and a preserving sweet."

"How beautiful. You are indeed a poet, Mr. Wickersham."

Doffing his hat, he gave a stately bow. "No, dear child. I quote from Shakespeare's Romeo to his beloved Juliet, act 1, scene 1."

CHAPTER FIVE

Inside the house, Betty Ann sat Wickersham at the kitchen table and started preparing coffee. "Maybe I'll check on Dragonfly." Mark said. "It's been a couple of hours." Behind Wickersham, Ted put his finger to his lips and frowned. Mark saw the warning signal. Quickly, he said, "You remember, Ted? That neat computer game I was playing."

Ted followed Mark into the computer room and said sternly, "Don't you trust that old ham. He's hiding something." Bringing up the e-mail screen, Mark nodded absentmindedly and Ted turned to leave. "I'm gonna keep an eye on him."

Down the hall, Ted could hear Betty Ann, as she cooed to her latest houseguest. Approaching closer, he listened as she said, "And you came all the way from England, just to see our southern states?"

"'Tis true, dear lady."

"And for no other reason. That's so flattering."

"To say thus would a falsehood be, an untruth of dastardly proportions and a loathsome prevarication."

"Mercy, that doesn't sound good at all! What ever could be as bad as all that?"

Ted quietly stopped in the hall just around the corner.

"I dare not say, dear lady. Only that, for me, should morning not arrive, grieve not my passing. Surely Satan's pike has skewered my soul in hell ... and rightly so."

"Mercy! What in the world have you done to make you feel that way?"

"If I could but unburden my troubled spirit, dear lady, I would better be. Alas, I have sworn an oath of silence."

"Oh, you can tell me, Mr. Wickersham."

"Nay child, my pledge is like a rock."

"You are being awfully hard on yourself. I don't believe I could live up to such demands."

Ted turned and walked quietly back down the hall to the computer room leaving them alone. "Found anything?" he asked, looking over Mark's shoulder.

Mark said casually, "Nothing helpful. "Dragonfly says the funny marks are definitely encryptions."

After watching Mark at the keyboard for a while, Ted said, "Can he unscramble 'em?"

"He's working on it. He'll let me know."

Just then, Betty Ann came into the room. Hearing their conversation, she said, "What if he finds out that there's money involved, Mark? He may become greedy."

"I don't think so, Betty Ann, besides he doesn't have the figures. All he has are the encryptions and I swore him to secrecy."

"Well, he didn't keep your last secret, you know."

"He apologized for that when I told him about what happened today."

"This is getting really dangerous, Mark," she said, glancing at Ted, who had gone back to the door and was looking back up the hallway. "Those people that shot at us might find him."

Suddenly, Ted asked, "Where's Wickersham?"

"He's watching television, Ted. Don't worry about him. He's just an old Teddy Bear."

Mark keyed in a different account. "Don't think money's what makes Dragonfly tick."

Ted frowned. "You believe him?"

"He's a hacker, Ted, hooked on challenge."

Ted peered into the screen curiously. "Sure makes me tick."

"Well, I'll admit, I've thought about transferring a few million into an off shore account somewhere." He turned in the swivel chair and grinned. "But that's all it is, just a fantasy. Besides, I wouldn't even know how to do it." Suddenly, the flash-mail screen came to life. "Dragonfly's done it," Mark said excitedly. "Broke the code!"

"What do all those little thing-a-ma-jigs say?"

"They're names and account numbers, Betty Ann, just like I thought."

"Who's?"

"Look for yourself. He's decoded two. One guy's Benny Barbados."

Ted frowned, "The drug dealer?"

"That's right!" Betty Ann said, her eyes growing bigger. "Plea-bargain Benny! Last year he was in the paper every day or so. They were trying him for money laundering."

"Never served a day."

"Why was that?" Mark asked.

"Witnesses all disappeared."

"Dead most likely." Betty Ann's worried eyes fixed on Mark, a warning in her voice. "This is the kind of people you're mixed up with." She leaned over his shoulder and stared at the screen. "Who's that other name, Mark?"

"Some guy named Felix Fluggy," he said, looking puzzled. "Never heard of him, though."

Ted, scowled at the screen. "He's a cop."

"A cop!"

Betty Ann exclaimed, "I remember now, from New York City." Her eyes grew even larger. "There was something about him on TV a while back. They tried to convict him of taking bribes." She giggled nervously. "The press called him Flatfoot Fluggy. They dropped the case when he disappeared." Betty Ann glanced apprehensively at Ted. "He had the same lawyer that the mob used."

The three stared at the glowing screen for several minutes. When it became apparent that Dragonfly had no more information to send, Mark asked, "Think by now the limo driver's stopped looking?"

"I certainly hope so, Mark."

"Good. There are things I need to do and I may need your help."

CHAPTER SIX

The next morning Betty Ann was busily preparing breakfast. "I can't believe I left my purse in that office yesterday, Ted. It had all my credit cards, house keys, and my money."

"Uh-huh," he grunted without looking up from the newspaper he was reading.

"I need it back, Ted. Shouldn't I report it to the police?"

"No."

"Then, would you check with Walpole at the hospital?"

Reluctantly, Ted picked up the telephone and dialed the hospital number. After asking several questions, he listened for a few minutes than hung up. "Walpole's checked out!"

"Can you believe that? The way he was yelling when the ambulance pulled away, you'd think he'd be there for a week, at least. Call him at his home."

After looking through the telephone book, Ted dropped it on the table. "Not listed."

"We're almost out of grocery money, Ted."

Suddenly, the phone rang. Ted picked up the receiver and put it to his ear. "Yeah." After a pause he said, "Yeah, she just asked about it." There was another pause then he said, "All day." His eyebrows squinting suspiciously, he said, "Yeah, that's our number." Then he hung up.

Taking biscuits out the oven, she asked, "Who was that?"

Ted stared thoughtfully at the tablecloth. "Walpole."

"He called us?"

"Said he'd found your purse."

"Well where is he? When can we get it?"

"He's bringing it by the house."

"He sure recovered fast," she said. "Odd, he's bringing it all the way out here."

"Asked us to wait for him here."

Abruptly, Mark rushed into the room, looking worried. "There's something you should see ... on TV." They went into the living room. "Damn, you're too late." His frightened words spilled out in one long burst. "Showed a picture of the man killed in town, the one with the gun. He's a hit man for the mob! The question they're asking is ... who was he after?"

"If it was you," Ted said, glancing at Betty Ann to see how she was taking it, "can't hurt you anymore."

"But what about the others, Ted? That's what worries me."

"Mercy! He was after you, Mark?" The frightened look on his face answered her question. "Oh, Mark!"

"How did they find me so quick?"

Betty Ann put a comforting arm around Mark's shoulder. "Well you're safe here with us. Ted won't let anything happen."

"How'd I get in such a mess?"

Betty Ann gave him a motherly hug. "Now, now, Mark. Stop worrying. You're safe now. Go wake up Mr. Wickersham. Let's have some breakfast before these biscuits get cold.

Two hours after breakfast and still no sign of Walpole, Betty Ann began to fret. "Maybe he's not coming, Ted."

"Said he would."

"Well where is he then? Maybe he can't find our house."

"Has the number."

The afternoon dragged by slowly. Suppertime came and went. Ted and Wickersham played gin rummy while Betty Ann loaded supper dishes into the washer. Mark peered out though the front window into the dark. "I don't think he's coming."

When Wickersham cried Gin, Ted dropped his cards on the table in disgust. "Betty Ann, we need to talk."

She dried her hands on the apron around her waist, then removed it and hung it on a hook in the closet. Grinning at him, she said, "All right, lover." Arm in arm, they walked out onto the long front porch.

Protected by a wide roof that blocked them from a distant street light, they sat on the porch swing in the deep shadows. The fragrance of Honeysuckle Roses filled the summer breeze. They huddled together, speaking quietly. Ted said, "We need that money in your handbag."

"Yes, I know. Our house guests are eating everything in sight."

"Keep your voice down, Doll."

Lowering her voice even more, she said, "They can't hear us, Ted." She reached over and took his hand. "They'll be gone soon, darling. In a way, this has been fun, don't you think?"

Glancing at her, he almost missed the movement in the yard across the street. Squeezing her hand to get her attention, he said, "Look!" They watched as a match flared near the front door.

"He's looking for a number; Walpole's finally come." Betty Ann said and attempted to stand.

Ted, still holding her hand, pulled her back down. "Shush, that guy's tall ... Walpole's short."

From the shadowy porch, they heard a faint high pitched whistle and the dark figure turned back and crossed to the other side just as a long black limousine came into view. "A voice beside the limo growled, "That's the house."

Ted held Betty Ann's hand in a tight grip. "Don't move!" he whispered. Across the street a figure emerged from deep shadows. They watched it race to the waiting limo. Soon, two more figures appeared and ran to the car. With a soft sound, the car door closed behind them, and the limo sped away. Ted relaxed.

"That's the same car!" Betty Ann said. "What were ..." Suddenly, there was an explosion. The neighborhood shook as the house across the street turned into a fireball. Betty Ann stared transfixed as flames reached toward the treetops.

Mark ran out onto the porch, his face looking pail in the yellowish glow. "Would you look at that!" he said. "What happened?"

"That black limo came back," Betty Ann said.

Wickersham followed them out. His eyebrows knitted. "It is the bright day that brings forth the adder, and that craves wary walking. Brutus said as much in Julius Caesar, act 2, scene 1."

"He got that right!" Ted pushed the three back through the front door. "They're a bunch of snakes all right." Quickly he shut the door. "All lights off and keep out of sight. They'll be back."

Mark stared through the window at the blazing building, "Why that house?"

"They got the wrong one, Mark," Betty Ann said, trying to appear calm for Mark's sake. "It was a mistake."

"The wrong house!" He began to tremble as it sunk in. "That was meant for me, wasn't it!" Watching through the window, early onlookers, like sea birds scampering ahead of a wave, moved back into their front yard, avoiding fire trucks pulling up across the street. "How could that happen, Betty Ann?"

"Numbers messed up, Mark." She put a comforting hand on his shoulder. "That house had our number on it."

"I knew Walpole was a sleaze ball, but he wouldn't do something like this, would he? This is murder! What would he have to gain?"

"Now Mark, didn't you say you told him about your password thing?"

"But he didn't seem interested, Betty Ann."

"Maybe they offered him money."

"And he set us up to be murdered for money?"

"He had our phone number," Ted growled. "They got to him."

"Yes, Mark," Betty Ann said quietly. "Otherwise, why would he call, asking us to wait here?"

"So we'd be in the house!"

"Exactly."

"But he doesn't even know I'm here."

"How do you know that, Mark?" Betty Ann said, patiently. "The limo driver saw you in our car. Maybe they ran our license tag number."

"Oh God! What have I got you mixed up in?"

Through the window in the darkened front room, Wickersham watched over Mark's shoulder at the people milling about. His face accentuated by the inferno he said solemnly, "The plot thickens."

Suddenly, Ted pulled them back from the window. "They're back!" Following a solid line of curious sightseers, the black limo passed slowly by.

"Egad, in their place, I would but fear the inevitable hand of yon constable upon my quaking shoulder. Audacity such as this suggests an even more fiendish scenario. Perchance, some mysterious concealment, yet unrevealed."

An hour later, the acrid odor of burnt timbers still penetrated the house. Ted and Betty Ann sat watching the late news on television. The fire across the street had finally been extinguished. Wickersham sat in a rocking chair, snoring quietly and Mark had gone to bed. Betty Ann yawned and stretched. "I'm turning in, Ted. They're not going to show us anything more tonight." Suddenly, she jumped as the phone jingled loudly in the quiet house. "Who would be calling this time of night?"

"Don't answer it," Ted said.

Betty Ann fidgeted, listening to the persistent ringing. After the fourth ring she jumped up. "Can't stand it Ted. I've got to know." She picked up the phone, and in a sleepy sounding voice, she said, "Hello."

"Is this the home of Betty Ann Beezly?"

"Who's calling at such a late hour?"

"Is this the home of Betty Ann Beezly?" the voice asked again, this time sounding vaguely familiar. "I got to speak to her. It's a matter of life or death."

"You have your nerve," she said with as much indignation as she could muster, "waking me up at this ungodly hour. There's no one here by that name!" Her hand shook as she placed the phone back onto the cradle.

"Who was that?"

"I don't know," she said, staring at the telephone. "A man's voice asked to speak to me."

She began to pace the floor. "Ted, that voice? It sounded vaguely familiar! Nasal and whiny, with a slight lisp?"

"Walpole?"

"Yes, how did you know?"

"Just a guess." Ted watched Betty Ann, as she turned it over in her mind.

Then the phone rang again. "I'll take this one," Ted said angrily. "Hello." He listened for several seconds. "Yeah, okay," he said gruffly. Turning his back to Betty Ann, so she couldn't hear the conversation, he spoke for a minute more, then hung up. Betty Ann studied his expression, trying to read his thoughts. His eyes were darting back and forth, his mind racing.

"Well, Ted, Are you going to tell me or not?"

"It *was* Walpole."

"I thought so!"

"Apologized for not showing."

"What possible excuse did he have?"

"Said he'd explain."

"Explain? When?"

"When I see him."

"You didn't invite him here, did you?"

"No."

"You're going to meet with him somewhere?"

Ted's expression became grim. "Uh-huh."

"When, for God sake, Ted?"

"Now."

She saw the determined look on his face. "No, Ted. Don't. You know it's a trap!"

"Got to."

"No you don't," she said angrily. "This is just like it was back in that old war you were in ... all that killing. It's what you were trained for ... and you loved the excitement of it!"

"Gotta go."

Defeated, she sat back in her chair. "Where does he want you to meet him?"

"Under Wingate stoplight."

"Don't do it, Ted. Please!"

"He's bringing your purse."

"I don't care," she said, grabbing hold of his arm. "Stay here with me, please don't go."

He gently removed her hand. "I'm going, Betty Ann."

"I could never talk you out of anything," she whimpered, turning her face away from him. Then, she turned back, "Please be careful Ted, I need you."

"Plan to." Wickersham, still in the chair, snored quietly, as Ted slipped out into the night.

CHAPTER SEVEN

Like a phantom, he tiptoed through the dark college campus, and across a wooded field. Standing in the shadows, Ted searched the area around the Klondike. Except for a barking dog, there was no sign of life. Then he saw movement near the building. The figure limped out and peered up and down the highway, then disappeared back into the shadows behind the building.

Ted crossed the street, keeping the Klondike between them. Satisfied that there was no one else there, he walked quietly down beside the restaurant, and slipped into the shadows of the parking lot. Walpole, he could see, was hiding in the shadows at the far corner biting his fingernails.

Quietly, Ted slipped up behind the little man. "You looking for me?" His voice sounded deep and accusing.

"Oh shit!" Walpole yelled and started to run.

"Wait up, you called me, remember?"

He stopped and turned around. "Ted? Where da hell did you come from?" Limping back, he whined, "You move like a frigging ghost."

"You have something for me?" Ted growled.

"I'm taking a big chance doing dis, you know."

Ted put his hand out. "The handbag?"

"I hid it," Walpole whined nervously. "Don't worry, its close by."

"Get it."

"First, I got a question."

"Yeah?"

"Yeah. Where'd you drop off my client?"

"Who's your client?"

"You know, Mark what's-his-face. Da kid dat was in my office."

"Didn't drop him. Now, give."

"Don't hand me dat crap. You've been seen together."

"Who says?"

"People."

"Now *I've* got a question." Ted leaned in closer. "You with those people?"

"What people?"

"That burned down the house?"

"I don't know nothin' 'bout no fire," Walpole said, backing out of Ted's reach.

Ted stepped closer. "You with the mob?"

"I'm not working wit' no frigging gangsters! I ain't *dat* dumb." Limping past Ted, Walpole peered around the corner, nervously searching the street beyond. "Da ting's dis way. You coming?"

"Right behind you." Ted followed him along the sidewalk in front of the Klondike, around a telephone pole planted in the sidewalk beside the curb.

"We're *reel* close." Stopping, Walpole turned back toward Ted. "Well where is he?"

"Took him to the hospital," Ted lied.

"Was he hurt?"

"No. To visit you."

"I must of missed him," he whined. "Somebody else got there first." Walpole stopped at the door. "My hip was dislocated." He leaned against the wall, obviously in pain. "It's better now."

"Where's the damned bag?" Ted growled. "I don't have all night."

"What's your hurry?"

Ted grabbed his lapel and pulled him in close. "Get it now."

The shirt started to rip. "Hey, watch-it! It's inside da screen door."

"Just like that?"

"If you didn't show, I planned on leaving it … let somebody else deliver it."

Ted quickly opened the screen and picked it up. Under the street light he examined the contents. "Billfold's missing!"

"Sheesh, I didn't look inside da bag. That guy at the hospital handed it to me, along with half of a C-note. Said I'd get da other half when I delivered it to you."

Suddenly, Ted saw car lights come on a half block away. "Hell, who's that?"

"What?" Walpole said, looking past him down the highway.

"I think you're friends are back." A truck, its gears whining as it picked up speed, came speeding toward them fast.

"Day said day wouldn't try nothin'!"

Ted began running back down the sidewalk. "And you believed 'em?" he yelled.

Walpole's short legs moved twice as fast as Ted's. He quickly caught up and was close on Ted's heels when the stolen UPS truck swerved over the curb onto the narrow sidewalk. It scraped along the restaurant wall, sparks flying, heading directly at the two running figures.

"Oh shit!" Walpole yelled, as the truck bore down. Just before it reached them, Ted pulled Walpole behind the telephone pole planted in the cement walkway and the truck swerved to avoid it. Sideswiping the post, the truck tipped over onto its side. Skidding in a slow spin, it came to rest in the middle of the highway. "Day tried to *kill* me!" Walpole yelled as he ran behind the building into the shadowy parking lot. Someone began forcing the passenger door open. Then a man climbed out and reached back inside. His hand came up holding something long and dark.

Ted said, "That's a shotgun."

"Yeah, and dis ain't quail season."

After, putting distance between them and the UPS truck, they doubled back into the safety of the college campus. Under stately oaks, they raced along well-worn walkways that crisscrossed over manicured lawns. Dormitory buildings loomed around them in the darkness. Here and there, a dimly lit window gave testimony to a late night study session.

Ted stopped beneath a dormitory window beside of series of steps and searched the gloom behind them. Walpole sat down on the cement staircase to catch his breath. Reaching in his pocket he removed a package. Shaking a cigar out, he put it to his lips. Ted knocked it away.

"Hey, watch it! Dat's a Cuban." He picked it off the ground and slipped it back in the package. "Sheesh, deeze tings cost money you know. Don't you smoke?"

"The match, stupid. He'd see it."

"Oh," Walpole said, looking back in the direction that they had just come from. "See anyting?"

"Think we lost him."

Walpole relaxed and sat back down. "Tanks, guess I owe you one," he said, apologetically. "Day was after me, too, you know."

"Figured that out, did you?" Still watching the back trail, Ted said casually. "What else you doing for 'em?"

"Day was paying me to get somethin' ... dat's all."

"A floppy disk?"

"How did you know dat?"

"Because I have it," Ted lied.

"Sure you do."

"Grabbed it off your desk ... when you scampered down the hall."

"I'll be damned! Day been after da wrong one all along." Standing up, he pulled a pistol from a side pocket, and held it low on his hip like a grade B wild-west gunfighter. Ted recognized the silver-plated weapon at once.

"You going to use that thing?" Ted said angrily. "You've pointed it at me before."

"Not unless I frigging has to." Walpole began breathing harder, his eyes bright with excitement. Cocking the hammer, he said, "Now hand over da merchandise."

"After all I did for you?" Ted said. He reached in his back pocket as though searching for the disk. "Kept that truck from smashing you ... like the little worm you are." He moved another step closer. "And this is the thanks I get?"

"So what? We're talkin' mega-bucks here." Walpole sneered, as he placed the cigar back between his curled lips and struck a match on the pistol barrel. The wooden stick flared brightly and he inhaled in the smoke. "With that kind of loot, I already forgot you saved my ass." He blew a noxious cloud into Ted's face and grinned. "This'll put me right wit dem, too."

"Would you look at that? I don't have it on me." Ted eased another step closer. "Must of lost it."

Walpole lowered the pistol back to his hip. "Yeah? Where did ya loose it, Donkey-breath?"

"In my car, maybe." Walpole pulled on the panatela again. It glowed in his greedy little eyes.

"Where would dat be?"

"Now you're getting personal," Ted said evilly. "Don't know you that well."

Suddenly, the decorative shrubbery near the building parted and the man with the shotgun stepped out. He had the hard-muscled look of a weight lifter. "Good work, short stuff" he said. "Led me right to him."

Walpole looked rattled. "You saw my signal?"

"Yeah. You'll get a bonus for this."

Ted quickly sized up the situation. "Yeah. It'll be a bullet in your ear." His cynical grin returned. "You know too much, already."

"What?" Walpole said, suddenly comprehending. He dropped the pistol behind him on the ground.

"You're just a pawn." Ted said grinning evilly. "An expendable chump."

"A lot you know." Walpole's lip curled until his teeth were showing. "These guys will take care of me. They *need* me."

"What makes you think that?" the gunman said, an amused look on his face.

"Cause I know who's got dat disk you're after."

"Oh? I'm listening."

Walpole looked pleased with himself. He pointed a thumb over his shoulder at Ted. "Dis guy has it. He told me so."

The thug pointed the shotgun at Ted. "Give," he said. "Now!"

With his eyes locked on the gunman, Ted said, "Wrong move, Walpole. They already tried to kill you once. After this they won't need you anymore." With the grace of a dancer, the hit man moved closer to Ted and shoved the weapon against his chest "You're pretty good," Ted said. "How'd you find us?"

"Shut up. Give me the disk?"

"I was watching our back trail. You didn't follow us."

The gunman leered at Ted. "The shrimp has a bug in his pocket."

"The hell you say!" Walpole felt around in his breast pocket and came up with the device. "You never said nothin' about no bug! Damn! You said you trusted me!"

"Shut up." He focused on Ted. "No more delays. Give me the disk, NOW."

Ted held his hands high in the air. "I gave it to him," he said nodding in Walpole's direction.

"You're crazy!" Walpole's eyebrow began to twitch. "You didn't give me nothin' but grief. I don't has it!"

"He's got it," Ted said. "Frisk him."

Suddenly the man in black turned toward Walpole and growled, "Turn your pockets out. All of 'em."

"I don't has the frigging ting! He's lying, I tell you!"

"Do it now, or I'll search your dead body."

"All right, all right." Walpole emptied one pocket after another. "I'm supposed to be on your side, you know." With his pockets turned out, he stood still while the gunman inspected every possible hiding place.

"Now you," he said, pointing the shotgun back at Ted.

"He must have hidden it someplace, after I gave it to him," Ted's voice became higher, accusing. "Somewhere near the restaurant."

"He never gave me a frigging ting." Beads of sweat began to pop out on the little detective's forehead. "Can't you see he's lying?"

The gunman turned back toward Walpole. "I know your track record, shrimp. Where'd you hide it?"

Walpole glared at Ted. "He said he left it in his car! I ain't got da damned ting!"

"We'll double the stakes, if you tell me now. You'll never have to work again."

"He's right," Ted said quietly taking a step closer. "Dead people never have to work much."

"Shut up," the hit man said. Turning back, he jabbed the gun muzzle hard into Ted's stomach. Out of the corner of his eye, Ted watched Walpole back away. Then the thug cocked the hammer. "You first. Then he gets it next," he said, glancing back at the spot where Walpole had been standing.

Suddenly, Ted made his move. Pushing the barrel off to one side, with a quick twist, he wrenched it out of the gangster's hand. The blast was deafening and a window nearby exploded into slivers of glass. "Now stand real still," Ted said, as lights appeared in several dormitory windows. "There's always the other barrel."

"You're quick," the hit man said, shifting his body away from Ted. "That was a good move." Suddenly, with speed so fast Ted couldn't react, he found himself flying through the air, the weapon no longer in his hand. Landing on his back, Ted rolled to one side and almost made it to his feet, when the blow from a soft leather shoe hit his face. He fell back on his butt and shook cobwebs from his head as he rolled over and came to rest on one knee. "Now give me the disk?"

"I told you, Walpole has it." Ted ducked the kick aimed at his head. Instead it landed on his shoulder and he fell flat on his back.

"This is getting nowhere," the gunman said, quickly picking up his shotgun. "I'll find it my way." He pointed the gun at Ted's head. Ted held his breath, waiting for the explosion.

CHAPTER EIGHT

The loud noise echoed off campus walls. Abruptly, an expression of disbelief came on the gangster's face. He slumped to the ground revealing Walpole standing behind his back holding the silver-plated pistol. Walpole glared down at the body on the ground. "I'm changing sides, scum-bag." Overcome with excitement, he pranced around waving the pistol in the air. "I'm too young to die. Haven't seen Gone Wit Da Wind yet." He squatted beside the hood and felt for a pulse.

"Is he dead?" Ted asked, getting to his feet.

"You frigging better believe it. I couldn't of missed from up dis close." Picking up the little tracking device, Walpole stuck it under the gangster's belt. "Now day can track him all da way to hell."

"You sure nailed him."

People began to pour out of the surrounding buildings, and Ted started back toward the Klondike at a fast clip. Sirens wailed in the distance as Walpole ran to catch up. "What now?" Ted asked, eyeing the pistol in his hand. "Aren't you gonna wait and tell the police what happened?"

"Cops and me don't get along; day gonna be here any second."

"Figured that out all by yourself?"

Walpole's lower lip curled. "Don't be such a wise ass."

Ted picked up the pace. "Don't follow me."

"I'm not. I'm just traveling da same direction as you."

"Find another direction."

"That's da tanks I get. I saved your ass back there. Now I can't even walk wit you?"

"And I saved yours; we're even."

The little man struggled to keep up with Ted's fast pace. "Sheesh, slow down some, can't-cha? I'm on your side, you know."

"Funny way of showing it."

"Dem guys had me 'tween a rock and a hard place, know what I mean?"

"How's that?"

"Needed da money. Word on da street was out dat people was spreading hard cash around for information."

"So?"

"So I gave 'em some ... and day gave me some."

"And you told 'em about Mark's little secret."

"Not at first. They bought some different bull. Paid me plenty, too."

"What about your oath to your client?"

"I never said at all costs."

"I'll tell him that, next time I see him."

"I was just trying to get ahead," he whined, "Dat's all."

"Aren't we all." Ted turned the corner and started down Main Street. Looking over his shoulder he could see blue lights flashing and the campus filling with people.

Walpole had to trot, to keep up. "All right, I admit I was in wit 'em, but nobody was supposed to get shot at."

Walpole began to lag behind. Ted slowed his pace and looked over his shoulder. "It was just for the money?"

Walpole nodded his head. "If da find us now, we'll both be dead meat."

"Pretty cold-blooded. Shooting him in the back," Ted said. "They'll know you turned."

"Yeah, I know," Walpole said, dejectedly. "Why was you in my office, anyway?"

"Heard you had connections."

"What kind?"

"With police."

"Boy, do you got dat wrong."

"Too bad," Ted said, starting to walk faster again.

"Course, I got a brother in Charlotte. He knows people on da force."

Ted slowed his pace again. "That's better."

"What's better about dat?"

Ted stopped and faced him. "I need information."

"What *kind* of information?"

"The kind he can get for me."

"Like what?"

"Never mind," Ted said. "Can't trust you"

"Me? Everybody trusts me. Ask anybody."

Ted laughed mirthlessly then thought about it for a minute, "Guess I'll have to."

"Yeah?" Walpole said. "What you lookin' for?"

"Answers."

"What kind of answers?"

"Are cops looking for someone."

"Oh? He can do dat, but it's gonna cost you."

"How much?"

"A couple of bills."

"I can handle that."

"Den it's a piece of cake."

Ted stopped and turned, his eyes accusing. "That's what you told Mark, wasn't it?"

"So he *is* wit you!"

Ted glared at him. "Didn't say that."

They walked along in silence. The only sound was that of Walpole's labored breathing. Finally Walpole said, "Guess I really am one of you guys, now."

"Hell you are!" Ted picked up the pace. "Got enough troubles."

"But, Mark still needs me."

Chuckling, Ted said, "I'll tell him that ... if I see him."

"Look," Walpole said, sounding sincere, "Mark's a good kid. I'm trying ta make it up to him for what I done."

"Sure you are," Ted chuckled cynically. "Sell your mother, for the right price." He stepped into a pay-phone booth. "Stay here," he growled, shutting the door in Walpole's face. After several rings, Betty Ann picked up on the other end. "It's me." He glanced out at Walpole, making sure he couldn't hear the conversation. "Walpole saved my butt tonight."

"He's with you now?"

"Yeah. Here's what I want you to do." He talked for several minutes, than hung up. Opening the door, he looked down at Walpole who was chewing on an unlit cigar. "Any more bugs?"

"Sheesh, you wonna search me?"

"Nope." Ted pulled him into an passageway beside the phone booth. "We'd better wait in here." The silver plated pistol in Walpole's hand gleamed in the dark. "Hand over the piece."

"Here, take it. But, remember where ya got it, Pal," he whined. "I'll be asking for it back."

"I'm not your pal." Ted pulled out a handkerchief. "Got to blindfold you."

"Hey! I'm on your side now, remember?"

"Just in case." An ugly grin on his face, Ted mumbled, "Wouldn't want to put temptation in your path."

"You frigging still don't trust me!"

Ted began to roll up a handkerchief. "See it from my side." Before he could tie it, auto headlights momentarily erased the shadows as a car turned the corner a block away. It slowly moved down the dark street toward them. Ted dragged Walpole deeper into the alleyway and they hid behind a Dumpster. "Dat a limo?" he asked tensely, searching for a way out of the dead end street. Walpole began to shake and his eye twitch came back. "Can't tell from here." He huddled behind the Dumpster, trying to make himself invisible. "Dem guys will kill us witout tinkin' twice. There're bad freaking dudes."

Grabbing Walpole by the throat, Ted growled, "You sure there's no more bugs?"

"Hell yes, I'd of known." Suddenly, the car pulled into the alley and stopped. Powerful headlights lit up the passageway. Walpole's body went tense. Panting, he suddenly jerked free of Ted's grip and scampered out toward the blinding light. "Don't shoot ... it's me!" he yelled hysterically, "it's me, it's me!"

The car door slowly opened and a figure stepped out. Walpole flung himself to the ground and covered his head. Walking over, Ted grabbed him by the arm and lifted him to his feet. "You changed sides real quick."

"Sheesh, I taught it was dem. Dat scared da crap out of me."

"It was a test," Ted chuckled. "You flunked."

His eyes still wild, he stammered, "But day was coming to kill us!"

Betty Ann stepped out into the glare of the headlights and began to laugh. "Mercy, that was funny," she wiped tears from her eyes. "Sorry we frightened you Mr. Walpole, but we just had to know."

"Don't ever do dat again," Walpole said. He began wiping sweat from his face with his handkerchief. "I could of had a frigging heart attack."

"Cut the language," Ted growled. "That's a lady you're talking to. Do it again and I'll pinch your head off."

"Sheesh, no offense. All da broads I know is used to it."

Ted made sure the blindfold was secured. Driving Matilda in a roundabout way, he made the two-minute journey to the house in just under fifteen. In the backyard, he parked the car out of sight against the hedgerow. "Do what I told you, Doll?" Betty Ann nodded, enjoying the game. "Take the blinders off, then." Inside, all publications that had their address on them had been removed.

Betty Ann led Walpole down the hallway. "You don't mind sleeping in a bathtub, do you?" Walpole rolled his eyes at her, but said nothing.

Walking through a bedroom, Ted opened a bathroom door. "Only way out is past me." He grinned evilly. "Since I acquired this pistol," he said, winking at Betty Ann. "I've developed a shoot first strategy."

Betty Ann brought in a blanket and a pillow and started making it into a bed. "We'll use the bathroom down the hall."

"Never slept in no tub before."

"You're gonna love it," Ted said. "Soft as a hospital bed."

"Yeah, I'll bet." Walpole looked contrite. "Right after I got to dat hospital, dem guys showed up. Spent da whole frig ... uh, a lot of time wit 'em ... going true da rubble ... lookin' for da disk."

"Why?"

"Day didn't say, but I figured out dat a lot of money was on da line. Dat's when I found da purse."

"So, why'd you have the disk in the first place?" Betty Ann asked, keeping him talking.

"Mark what's-his-name brung it to me. Said he just wanted me to give it back." Walpole's expression became sly and confidential. "My job was to find somebody at Corsair Enterprises to give it to."

"And you saw a way to get a little extra?"

"Yeah ... somethin' like dat," Walpole licked his lips. "When I called 'em, day offered me ten-large if I could produce it. Sent me a frig ... uh ... a tousand up front by special messenger."

"Well, that's what Mark wanted you to do, wasn't it?" she said, putting a sheet down on top of the blanket. "Give it back?"

He nodded. "Da messenger turned out to be two big bruisers wit guns and bad attitudes," He said, cringing at the thought. "After searching in what used to be my office, we figured dat he must of took it wit him."

"It was on your desk, remember?" Ted said.

"Sheesh, I couldn't tell 'em dat! Day took her billfold with her driver's license in it."

Betty Ann glanced knowingly at Ted. "And the house blew up after that."

Walpole looked apologetic. "Never told me day was gonna do any of dat stuff."

"Well," Betty Ann said, "if the disk was in there, now it's burnt to a cinder."

"Yeah. There goes my nine-large."

"It was just a come-on, Mr. Walpole. You would have never seen any of that money." Betty Ann placed a pillow on the makeshift bed. "It sounds to me like they were planning to kill you all along. All that trouble over a little old piece of plastic." She stood and looked at him reproachfully. "Ted told me you even killed someone over it tonight."

He rolled his eyes at Ted who shook his head and frowned. Walpole understood the signal. "It was him or me, lady."

"Mercy, why didn't you just run away?"

"Couldn't. He had a bug planted on me. I wouldn't of gotten very far."

"Yeah, that reminds me," Ted said, "how'd they do that?"

"There was tree of us in da back seat, see. Me and da two goons ... real crowded ... cozy like ... know what I mean? One goon had his arm around my shoulder." Walpole's nasal whinny voice became contrite and apologetic. "He must of planted it then." His fidgety hand wiped perspiration off his forehead. "They all said day trusted me ... day said I was one of dem! Who would of tought?"

"Yeah, who?" Ted said mirthlessly. "So how'd you get away?"

"Day told me to get out and give you another call. Dumped me across from dat Klondike place ... den day just drove off."

"And you fell for it," Betty Ann said. "It was a set-up?"

"You got dat right, lady." Anger crept into his whiney voice. "When I saw dat frig ... uh ... dat truck coming down da sidewalk at us, dat's when I knew for sure. I don't need dat kind of grief."

Walpole hovered over the tub, looking curiously at Betty Ann's creation. Two folded blankets for a mattress and a folded sheet on top of that with a couch-pillow completed the ensemble. She said, "You're lucky you're alive, you know that?"

"Does a Bear sh ... uh ... go in the woods?"

Ted glared at him.

"Uh ... yes ma'am ... lucky. If I ever see dat Mark what's-his-name again, I'll make sure he has some grief of his own."

Closing the bathroom door behind them, Ted said, "Let's keep him in the dark."

"Why, he seems sincere to me."

"Mob doesn't trust him; neither do I." He looked at Betty Ann, an amused expression on his face. "Tomorrow's gonna be interesting."

"Why?"

"Mark," he grinned.

Betty Ann giggled. "And he has no idea who is sleeping in the next room."

The next morning Ted rushed into the kitchen where Betty Ann was preparing breakfast. "Where's Wickersham?" His voice sounded agitated. "Not in the house."

She looked up and smiled. "He's been up for hours, Ted." Brushing an unruly strand of hair from her forehead, she opened the oven door and removed a tray of hot breakfast biscuits; their aroma filled the room. Placing them onto a serving tray, she licked a hot crumb from her finger. "Told me his life's story before he left." She smiled as she remembered the conversation. "Did you know he acquired that odd behavior while in a house of detention?"

"The Shakespeare thing?"

"Uh-huh. In England." Her eyes twinkled at him. "He was caught after he stole the cash box at a London theater during a performance of Hamlet. Ran on stage with it in his hand. The judge at his trial turned out to have been in the audience."

"So?"

"Wickersham yelled at the audience as he was being dragged away, 'What's the matter with you people, can't you speak English?'"

"Doesn't explain anything, Doll."

"Seems the judge had an ironic sense of humor, darling. Confined him, until his trial, in their local hoosegow ... which, incidentally, was right beside the theater's outdoor practice arena."

Ted picked up the morning paper. "Uh-huh," he said only half listening.

"While waiting for his trial, he made the mistake of complaining about the ridiculous language coming through his cell window from the practice yard."

He turned to the sports page. "Got their money back, didn't they?"

"That's not all," she said, giggling. "This is the funny part. When the judge heard about his complaint, his punishment was three months in the poky. And while there, he could only communicate by using lines from Shakespeare's plays."

Ted looked up from the sports page and grinned. "That's it?"

"He was given several volumes to read. Every time he expressed himself normally, another fifteen days was added to his sentence."

Ted dropped the paper on the table. "I'd still be in there."

"Every time he wanted something, he had to find a sentence in one of the plays that said what he needed to say. Then, after while he became so good at it that the judge let him out on work release to work in the theater."

"So that explains it."

She chuckled, "By the time he was released, he had a habit he couldn't or wouldn't break ... and a paying job as a Shakespearean actor."

"Where is he now?"

"Asked directions to the library. Guess he's over at the college."

At that moment, Walpole walked into the kitchen. His face looking as rumpled as his suit. "Dat's a first for me," he said. Then he noticed Ted. "Never slept in no frig ... uh ... no tub before. My back hurts like hell."

Betty Ann shook her finger at him. "Be thankful," she said. "If that truck had hit you, you'd be in the morgue right now."

"Yeah, and if dat little turkey, Mark what's-his-name, hadn't of got me mixed up in dis, I wouldn't be in dis mess a-tall."

"You took his money, then played both sides of the street. That wasn't very nice, Mr. Walpole."

"Sheesh, if I ever run into him again ..." Walpole's anger began to build. He held his hand out and clinched his fist as though squeezing something. "No tellin' what I'd do."

"You'd better run away? He's bigger than you."

"He's not dat much bigger. I'd pulverize him and feed his bones to my dog."

Mark walked in and heard the end of the conversation. Coming quietly up behind him, he put his hand on Walpole's shoulder. "Your dog, huh?"

Walpole wheeled around, eyes big as saucers. He stuttered, "Where ... where da hell did *you* come from?"

"Here's your chance," Mark said quietly. "Thought I could trust you."

Walpole slowly backed away. "You never said nothin' 'bout no heavy dudes. Just some nerdy computer freaks."

Mark followed him, staying in his face. "You were supposed to find a way to give the disk back without them knowing who I was."

Walpole whined, "Day twisted my arm ... *real* hard."

"Well, now you can tell 'em the disk is in a safe place."

"Where's dat?"

"Just tell 'em, if something happens to any of us ... like maybe an accident or something ... it goes to the IRS with a letter telling all the details."

Walpole's eyes grew shrewd. "You're too young to be dat smart."

"Try me."

"Day'll find you and get it away from you ... it won't be no picnic neither."

"You just tell 'em what I said." Mark shoved the private detective against the kitchen wall. "You tell 'em, if I'm killed, the IRS will get the first copy, then there'll be two more copies mailed out. There's enough to spread around to the FBI and I haven't figured out who else yet."

Walpole scooted out from under his arm and put a table between them. "I don't work for you no more."

Mark took a step toward him. "You don't work for me? What about all the money I've paid you?"

Walpole edged toward the kitchen door. "Dat was up front money; spent it investigating."

"You expect me to believe that?"

"Had to spread heavy green around to find a contact, didn't I?"

"And you sure found one ... the lowlife with the silencer?"

"Didn't know about dat guy ... 'till one of dem hoods said somethin' in the car ... while day was taking me over to dat Klondike joint." He edged closer to the door. "Said, if it hadn't been for dat twister, you'd be dead meat already."

"Yeah ... how'd they know I was there?"

"Must of followed me back. Couldn't of been too hard." Suddenly, Walpole ran for the door.

Ted stepped in front of him, blocking his path and grabbed him. "Stick around."

"Why? There ain't gonna be no drawin'."

He struggled, trying to pull loose, but Ted dragged him back to the kitchen table and sat him down roughly. "Stick around anyway."

"You can't hold me with out no warrant. Am I being kidnapped?"

Ted grinned evilly down at him. "Call it protective custody."

Suddenly, Betty Ann motioned Ted and Mark into the living room. In subdued tones, so that Walpole couldn't hear, she said, "I think we should get away from here fast. That limo just drove by again!"

Ted watched Walpole through the open door, making sure he stayed put. "Where can we go, Betty Ann?"

"We'll stay with Lizzy in Marshville. I called her when I thought we might have to run from those cutthroats. She said it would be okay."

"I don't know. There's three of us."

"Ted, I've known Lizzy for ever. She's my best friend and there's plenty of room at her house." Betty Ann glanced though the window again. "We'd better leave now before they come back."

"What about Wickersham?"

"I'll leave him a note, Ted." She picked up a pen and started to write. "I'll tell him he can stay here as long as he needs. They're not after him."

Mark pulled two floppies from his pocket. "I'll mail one to a friend and I'll keep one with me."

"Good." Ted tied Walpole's hands behind his back, and blindfolded him. Then he hustled him out the back door and shoved him into the car. Closing the door, he pulled Mark off to the side. "Betty Ann's going to let him off on the hill. She'll come back ... pick us up here."

"What's the hill?"

"A rough section. He won't like it."

Betty Ann got behind the wheel. Winking at Ted, she whispered in a loud enough voice for Walpole to hear, "Which side of the river do you want me to drop him? Deep or shallow?"

Walpole started at her words. He pulled frantically at his bonds. "Don't do nothin' rash. I can't swim!"

Stifling a laugh, she said, "Don't worry about that old river, Mr. Walpole. The fall from the bridge will probably be fatal." She waved merrily at Ted and pointed Matilda in the direction of the hill.

Thirty minutes later, Mark said, "She ought to be back by now, Ted. Maybe it's car trouble. She could be in a ditch someplace."

Ted looked bothered. "Matilda's okay."

"It's a pretty old car, you know."

"We'll wait."

An hour later, Mark's anxiety had increased. "Something's happened, Ted. You shouldn't have let her go."

"Get off my case," Ted growled. Pacing the floor, he muttered, "Let me think."

Still later, Mark stared out through the living room window into the dark. "She's not coming back, Ted ... they've got her."

Ted looked miserable. "If she could get to a phone, she'd call."

"They'll torture her, Ted!" Suddenly the phone rang, echoing through the still house. Mark jumped for it before Ted could pick it up. "Betty Ann? ..."

"What have you done with her? Let me speak ... yes, I'm all alone."

Ted reached for the phone and Mark held him at bay. "Are you all right, Betty Ann? Where are you? Betty Ann, can you hear me?" After another pause, Mark said dejectedly, "Let me speak to her again."

Ted put out his hand and whispered, "Give it to me."

Mark shook his head and put his finger to his lips. Suddenly, Ted lunged for the receiver. Mark, clutched it fiercely, keeping it to his ear. Through clinched teeth, he said, "If you hurt her, the FBI gets the disk. I'm not kidding." Again, Ted tried to wrench the phone from Mark's hand, but he pulled away and put a table between them. "I'll come alone. You better make sure she's not hurt."

Ted made another grab, as Mark hung up. "Why didn't you let me have the damned phone?"

"Told 'em I was alone, Ted. If they'd heard another voice, they'd know I was lying."

"Well, where is she?"

"I have no idea. There were noises in the background. Sounded like birds, maybe. We've got to help her, Ted. I didn't mean for her to get messed up in this."

"Think damn-it! Exactly what did she say?

"When I ask her where she was, all she said was the man is a tower. Why would she say that? It doesn't make any sense."

"That's all?"

"Yes, there was no time ... they didn't give her a chance to finish. Then the man came back on and said if I don't come alone and bring the disk, he'd feed her eyes to the birds."

Ted paused, his expression dark and unfathomable. "She's told us!"

"What?"

"She's at Wingate Tower."

"What is that, some kind of hotel?"

"Deserted grain silo ... private joke." Ted began pacing the floor again. "Pigeons! They're on the roof!"

"Where is it?"

"Edge of town."

"Yes, it could have been Pigeons I heard."

"When do you meet 'em?"

"Now. They said, come to the convenience store between here and Monroe."

"Tower's just down the road ... that fits."

"How will I get there, Ted? They have Matilda."

"Take a taxi ... drop me off first."

"They'll see you coming."

"It's dark ... I'll wear black."

"Ted, I'm afraid."

"It's the only way, Mark."

"But what if they ... "

"I'll be close by."

"They'll want the disk. What if ... ?"

"Give 'em a blank," he said, pushing Walpole's pistol into his belt. "If they get the real one, we have nothing else to deal with."

CHAPTER NINE

The shadowy figure scaled the chain link fence and slipped behind a boxcar parked on a side track, just as the limo headlights approached. It came to a stop along side the concrete building, and Mark stumbled out, his hands tied and his face covered by a hood. Two oversized gorillas pushed him toward the only door and they disappeared inside.

Ted quietly circled the smooth walls keeping in the shadows. From somewhere near the entrance a cigarette glowed. Reversing direction, he heard a distant shriek. Looking up he saw an opening several feet above his head and high above his head a figure dangled out over the side. Angling a board against the wall, he climbed up through the window, and found himself in an empty room.

Ted peeped around the corner of a door leading into the main chamber. No one was in sight. A red light flashed above a slatted elevator gate.

He quietly climbed over the gate into the elevator shaft and stood at the bottom looking up. Dim light filtered in through the several landing portals above his head. With barely enough space in the shaft the elevator car, far above, moved steadily upward.

Then just in time, he saw it. Coming toward him in the darkness was a huge flat counterbalance weight. On grease coated guide rails, like a giant guillotine, it sped down, between the slatted gate and the path that the elevator had taken.

Quickly, Ted flattened out against a utility ladder anchored to the adjacent wall. The heavy counterweight landed on its pad with a dull thud and simultaneously, the elevator car stopped on the top landing.

The ladder, wide rungs of steel anchored to the wall, extended to the roof just inches away from the gondola's path. Ted adjusted the pistol in his belt and started the long frightening climb. Halfway up, he heard Betty Ann scream, her voice sounding hollow in the tall shaft. He increased his speed. Then suddenly, the elevator car began to descend and far below, the huge counterweight started its return trip.

Not enough room! He thought, Reversing direction he rushed back down the ladder,. Without warning, the pistol in his belt came loose and fell. The gondola, was now so close that he could smell the rotting wood. There was no place to hide!

Then the elevator stopped at the landing just above his head. Someone stepped on board. Quickly, Ted squeezed into the tight space between the ladder rungs and the wall and the gondola glided past, only inches from his grease-smeared face. Through the wide cracks he saw the passenger inside. *He looks vaguely familiar.*

Betty Ann screamed again, pulling his attention away. He started toward the top once more. The counter weight silently moved up past him into its housing, and at ground level the gondola came to a stop.

At the top of the shaft, holding on to protruding bolts in the wall, Ted hand-walked across the giddy expanse and reached the gate beneath the counterbalance housing. He climbed over the barrier onto the flat roof.

Bathed in an eerie red glow from a partially broken neon sign, a scene of overturned barrels and shattered railings reminded him that strong winds had also been there. A loud thump, then another scream made him wince. He peeped around the corner, then ducked his head back. "Betty Ann!" he said under his breath. "Where's the others?"

Her wrists were secured to a railing and her ankles bound to a flagpole at her feet. Lying on her back tied spread eagle over a bulging canvas sack on the floor she still managed to cringe away from the hands of an unbelievably large man.

The giant, with cauliflower ears and a boxer's nose, muscles flexing in ham sized arms, while he fingered her hair. Betty Ann squealed, "Don't." On the floor next to her head, an injured pigeon fluttered helplessly near a fire ax buried deep in the wooden deck.

Ripping the ax loose, the ugly brute leaned over her, thrusting the sharp edge near her exposed throat. "Won't miss next time," he said, "next time." Touching the blade with his thumb, in a menacing whisper, he mouthed, "Pretty head fall off soft shoulders ... soft shoulders."

"Please," Betty Ann said. "I've told you what I know."

"You know," he said, the blade against her skin. "Better tell now ... tell now!"

She turned her face away, avoiding his determined eyes. "I don't know anything, I swear!"

"You'll tell ... 'fore night through ... you'll tell."

Tears came as she struggled against her bonds. "I don't know anything."

"Taste blade," he said, dragging it across her throat, "blade sharp."

"I can't tell you what I don't know!"

The crippled pigeon fluttered against his foot, distracting him. Reaching down, he snatched it up and shook it at her. "Tell me, or bird dies."

"Don't. You're hurting it."

"Tell now."

"I told you, the disk burned up. Someone set fire to our house."

"If you lie." He held the fluttering bird against the railing above her head. "THIS!"

The swift stroke loped off the bird's head and it fell onto her chest. Frantically, she shook her shoulders, trying to dislodge it, but the head lay there, its dead eyes staring at her. Mewing sounds came from her throat. "Get it off, Get it off!" she pleaded.

He grinned evilly at her. Holding the still fluttering body above her, he let blood spill onto her face and neck. "Talk now."

Ted slipped behind the support beam under the neon sign. On the far edge of the roof, someone was leaning out over the edge, looking down. In one hand, he held onto a rope that hung from a windlass jutting out over the edge. A pistol in his other hand was pressed into the rope.

Then, Ted saw Mark. He was seated on the floor resting against the railing, the hood still over his head and his hands still tied. *That guy first.*

The giant, busy with Betty Ann, didn't notice Ted, holding a length of two-by-four in his hand, as he tiptoed quietly over to the mobster leaning over the edge. The swift blow made no sound and the mobster fell silently over the edge, hitting the ground with a sickening thud. Quietly, Ted removed Mark's hood and untied his wrists. Putting a finger to his lips, he pointed at the giant, still leaning over Betty Ann.

Mark whispered, "They've gone to run the disk. Said they'd kill me if I tried to trick them."

"May not live 'til then," Ted said quietly, looking over the edge. There was Walpole hanging by his wrists at the end of the rope. With a gag firmly in his mouth, he looked up, eyes pleading. On the ground, the guard had heard the subdued thud and he wondered over.

"Betty Ann first," Ted whispered, "Need you Mark. See that Brute guarding her? This won't be easy."

"What can I do?"

"When I get his attention," he picked up the board, "hit him with this."

"When?" Mark said. "How will I know?"

"You'll know." Ted slipped nearer to the large man and hid behind the support beam again.

The monster, leaning over Betty Ann, was fondling her hair again. "Nice ... nice."

Betty Ann cringed. "Don't," she whimpered.

"See more," he said huskily, reaching for her belt, "more." He put his large hand on her stomach to hold her down. Betty Ann twisted and turned in an effort to keep him from unhooking her waistband. His eyes became veiled. "More ... Francis see more."

Gasping for air, Betty Ann squealed, "Get away from me you pig!"

"Not pig," he said. Drool dribbled from his half-opened mouth. Leering at her, he began unbuckling her belt. "See more!"

Ted picked up an empty hogshead and held the heavy cask over his head. Slipping up on the giant's blind side, he brought it down hard and it broke over his shoulders. The big man stood erect and turned around grinning. Nearly two feet taller than Ted, he scowled down at him. "Didn't hurt." Shaking broken pieces from his hair, he said again, "Didn't hurt." A puzzled expression came to his face. "Who you?"

"You'll find out." Ted said, lunging at him and butted him hard in the stomach. The giant grunted and laughed. "Didn't hurt ... didn't hurt"

Backing off, Ted searched for something that he could use to subdue the monster. The ax lay on the floor near Betty Ann. Ted made a lunge for it, but the giant reached it first. Holding the large ax as if it were a toy, he wagged a finger at Ted. "No, no, no." He pointed the wedge shaped blade at Ted who backed farther away. "Who you?"

"Easy with that," Ted growled, "Might hurt yourself."

"You not nice." Suddenly he brought the fire ax down, sinking it deep into the floor next to Betty Ann's face. "Be nice or Francis kill." His face became shrewd. "Kill her now."

"You don't want to do that," Ted said, circling him, knowing that the brute would keep facing him. "A mess to clean up."

"Be nice ... be nice."

"You're yellow," Ted said, probing for a weakness. "Killing a woman ... while she's tied up?"

"Kill her now," the giant warned. Raising the ax above his head, aiming at Betty Ann's throat. "Now!"

Betty Ann, said, "Be careful, Ted. He's strong as an ox."

"Dumb as one too." Ted took a step closer. "Come on dummy ... I'm not some defenseless girl." Moving still closer, Ted goaded him. "See if you can handle me."

Swiftly, in one continuous movement, the large man dropped the ax and grabbed Ted by the throat. Lifting him off the ground with one big hand, he grinned and pulled him in close. "That easy." Ted could smell his rotting teeth as he struggled helplessly. "You make Francis mad."

Without oxygen, Ted began to loose consciousness. Over the giant's shoulder, he could see Mark holding the board like a baseball bat, coming fast. "Make Francis mad," he said again, squeezing harder.

The board landed solidly, splintering against the giant's neck. The big man turned angrily in Mark's direction. "Didn't hurt ... didn't hurt."

The momentum of Mark's attack and the force of the blow catapulted him to within range. With his free hand, Francis grabbed Mark by his shirt. "What'd you do with Crawford?" Mark's feet dangled a foot off the floor. "Do with Crawford?"

"I don't know any Crawford."

"He guard you," Francis said, shaking Mark roughly, "guard you!"

"For God's sake, Mark, tell him." Betty Ann wailed. "He'll kill us all!"

"Crawford left," Mark said, eyeing Ted, who hung, limp as a broken shoelace, from the giant's hand.

"Not past me ... past me!"

Mark, jerked and twisted again, trying to free himself, but the giant held him easily. "Keep still, little boy or Francis hurt ... hurt you good."

Mark ceased struggling, and glanced at Ted, whose body had begun to twitch. Francis noticed it also and lowered Ted's feet to the floor, relaxing his grip slightly so Ted could catch his breath for a second. "You almost killed him," Mark said, "Now put me down."

"Uh-huh," the giant said, grinning, exposing crooked yellow teeth. "Now Francis hurt you." Suddenly, he slammed Ted and Mark together like a pair of cymbals. On impact, Ted came awake for an instant, then fainted again. Blood began to drip from Mark's nose. "Francis hurt more. Where Crawford?"

Feebly, Mark said, "He left!"

"Where's Crawford?" Francis said, hammering them together again. "Where Crawford?"

Betty Ann squirmed on the floor, trying to wiggle out of the ropes around her wrists. "Tell him, Mark. He'll kill you."

Mark looked at Ted for help, but he hung from the giant's hand, limp, bleeding and still. "You're going to kill us anyway," he muttered. "Crawford fell off the roof."

"Huh?"

"We pushed him. What do you think of that, you stupid bastard?"

Releasing his grip on Ted's neck, Francis dropped his unconscious body to the floor. "You killed Crawford!" Glaring evilly at Mark, he dragged him to the railing, and thrust him out over the edge. "Kill you now."

Then, from the elevator shaft the guard at the bottom yelled up, "Hey Francis, what's going on up there?"

Frustration on his face, he dragged Mark back onto the roof. At the elevator entrance, he yelled down defensively, "What?"

"Crawford's down here, Francis."

"Down there?" he said confusion in his voice, "Crawford up here."

"What's going on, Francis? He's dead ... fell off the roof."

Then suddenly the enormous man understood. "These fellers up here done it." He yelled, "they done it!"

"Can't you control a girl and a school boy and that little shrimp of a PI? I'm coming up with the Uzi!"

Desperation in his voice, Francis yelled down the shaft, "Don't worry, Red. Ain't no problem ... no problem." Red didn't answer. Francis leaned farther into the shaft and yelled again, "Ain't no problem, Red."

Without warning the elevator motor began to hum and the gondola started up the shaft. From out of its sheath, the counterbalance dropped like a guillotine. It hit Francis solidly on the shoulders and, holding onto Mark's shirt with a death grip, he tumbled over the edge.

Grabbing the gate, Mark hung on desperately. But Francis's heavy weight was too much for him. One by one, his fingers began to pull loose. "Help," he said weakly.

Suddenly, a hand grabbed his ankle. Digging his heels in, Ted stopped Mark's slide into space. As Mark's shirt tore loose, and the giant fell free, his voice echoed back up to them, "Didn't hurt ... didn't hurt." Then the sound of his body, hitting the gondola roof, came up the shaft.

CHAPTER TEN

"I thought he'd killed you, Ted!"

Ted heard the elevator motor. "It's still coming!"

Mark was already running to Betty Ann's side and started untying her. "Ted, someone's coming up here with a machine gun!" Mark yelled.

Betty Ann squealed. "Oh mercy!" Getting to her feet, she pulled her torn dress together. "That man was so big. In all my life I've never seen such a big one before."

"Never mind him, Mark said. "What do we do now?"

Ted yelled from the elevator door, "Hide somewhere, hurry!"

"What about you?"

"I'll think of something," he said as he climbed into the elevator shaft.

They searched for a place to hide among a profusion of empty hogsheads, some broken, some overturned and a few still standing. The shed, holding the motor and counter balance, stood close to the edge. "Hide out there," Betty Ann said, pointing at a two-foot ledge running around the corner of the building."

Mark eased out onto the narrow ledge and looked down. There was nothing but empty space between the ledge and the ground far below. "Nothing to hold onto." She handed him the ax. "That ... against a machine gun?"

"Can you think of something better?"

He hefted the large ax, weighing it in his hand. "If I can get close enough ... maybe."

"The ledge will only hold one, Mark. You've got to do it."

Hastily, Betty Ann turned a barrel broadside to the elevator door with the open end facing the narrow ledge, she climbed into it. "If he sticks his head inside, his back will be to you. Hit him with the ax, Mark. Don't miss."

Mark eased farther out onto the narrow ledge. "I'll try."

In the elevator shaft, Ted hand-walked the protruding bolts to the back side. Behind the ladder, he watched the gondola stop at the entrance and a swarthy man holding a machine-pistol stepped around something on the floor and walked out onto the rooftop. When he was out of sight, Ted peeped through a crack at the mess on the floor. "Hello Francis," he whispered. "Did it hurt?" Then he realized that the gondola completely blocked the entrance. "Francis made it through," he mumbled, as he quickly climbed to the top and dropped through the jagged hole that the giant had punched through the ceiling.

The gunman, his back to Ted, stood still, studying the profusion of overturned hogsheads. "I know use-is out here," he called out. "Come on out, use-guys."

Ted kept in the dark corner of the gondola and watched. "Can't tackle him," he thought, "he'd hear me coming."

Suddenly, the gunman pointed the weapon at a barrel on the other side near the windless and there was a long deafening explosion. Bullets streamed out, and the hogshead burst into shreds. "Better use-guys come out now!" Firing another long burst, he destroyed a second barrel. "Know what I mean?" He fired at a third barrel and it disintegrated into splinters.

The gunfire masked the sound of his footsteps as Ted slipped closer. He hid behind some machinery. *Still too far*, he said to himself.

The gunman stopped firing. "Better come on out. I know where you are."

Ted peeped over the top of his hiding place. His eyes widened. The swarthy gangster was looking at an overturned barrel close to the elevator shack. The edge of Betty Ann's dress had fallen out and was clearly visible. *Dumb place to hide*, Ted thought, getting ready to charge.

Instantly the gunman began running toward the barrel, firing as he went.

"No!" Ted yelled, as he sprinted after him, bullets puncturing the barrel, drowning out his words. Ted was almost on him when the dreadful noise stopped. Then the gangster heard Ted's footsteps. In slow motion the gunman turned and raised the weapon.

Without warning, Betty Ann stepped from behind the shed, wielding the ax above her head. She brought it down hard on the gunman's head. He spun back around, weapon firing in the air.

As he crumpled to the ground, Ted ran up. "That was too close," he said, picking up the weapon. "Thought you were in the barrel."

She fell into Ted's arms and began to cry. "That's what I wanted him to think."

"No time now. You can cry later."

Mark came out of hiding looking embarrassed. "Betty Ann had me hanging off the roof."

Ted grinned for the first time. "The roof?"

"It was the only way we could both hide in that small a space."

Betty Ann looked around. "Where's Mr. Walpole?"

"Probably still hanging over the edge," Mark said. "Do we bring him with us, Ted?"

"Leave him," he growled.

"No, Ted" Betty Ann said. "When they come back they'll kill him for sure."

Shrugging, Ted turned the Uzi over in his hand, inspecting it. "Better learn how to use this thing."

"Ted?"

"Okay, Doll, you and Mark get him up here fast."

Together they hauled Walpole back onto the rooftop and pulled the gag from his mouth. "Taught I was a goner for sure; my friggin' heart was in my throat, down there."

Betty Ann untied his hands. "We have to hurry."

As they approached the gondola, Ted was dragging Francis out onto the rooftop. Betty Ann leaned over and looked closely at the giant. She cautiously nudged him with her foot. "You sure he's dead?"

"Yeah, he's dead all right. "

"What a terrible way to die."

Ted grimaced, "Said it didn't hurt."

As they gathered in the gondola, Walpole looked up at the hole in the roof, "If dat fall didn't do it, da sudden stop sure did."

They exited the building and hid behind a freight car as an automobile came up the driveway. Two men got out and went into the silo. They heard the elevator motor humming and the gondola started toward the roof. Betty Ann whispered. "There's the chauffeur?"

Ted quietly sneaked over beside the limo. The driver sat blowing smoke rings through the open car window. Ted put the Uzi barrel against his neck. "No sound!" Quietly, Ted and Mark tied him up while Betty Ann placed a gag in his mouth. They left him on the ground and piled into the limo. Mark started it up.

From the roof, a flashlight beam shined down. Suddenly, bullets began to fly. Men were running on the silo roof as Mark drove the limo down the narrow dirt road. Bullets hit the top and whined away.

"Bullet proof!" Ted said. The limo reached the highway and when Mark turned it toward Wingate, Ted asked, "Where's Matilda?"

"Gas station," Betty Ann said. "Matilda was on empty. That's where they caught us."

"Pull over, Mark. I'm not leaving her." He slipped out into the night beside the highway, Uzi in hand. "Make sure this limo is hidden good when you get home. Meet you at the house." He walked across a dark field to where Matilda was parked. Placing the Uzi under a newspaper on the front seat, he walked over to the office.

Behind the cluttered counter, a motherly looking clerk in a soiled apron nonchalantly took his money. "Did you hear shooting a while back?" she asked. "Sounded like world war three was starting."

"Maybe firecrackers," Ted said as he hurried away. Back at Matilda he pumped gas, returned the nozzle, and got in behind the wheel just as a police cruiser pulled in behind him. Re-adjusting the newspaper over the Uzi, he mumbled, "Oh hell!"

The cruiser's door creaked open and country music blared out. A thickset County Sheriff struggled out from behind the wheel of an old Mercury, and ambled over. Under the paper, Ted's hand gripped the handle of the weapon, his finger on the trigger. The cop, breathing with some difficulty, shined his flashlight through the open window.

"Been watching this here car. Figured you'd come back fur-it."

"Something wrong, officer?"

Studying Ted's face suspiciously, he said, "Y'all not from around here, are ya?"

"Just moved to town. What's the problem?"

"Vehicle like this-un was seen speeding down River Road." His walleyed stare looked down suspiciously. "Motorizin' right along ... doing eighty, at least" He turned the light onto the back seat, then shined it into Ted's eyes again. "Was it you-ins doing all that motorizin'?"

"Not this here car, officer," Ted said, slowing his voice down, adopting the sheriff's red neck speech pattern, "Won't do sixty ... know what I mean?"

His flashlight beam moved to the front seat. "Yeah?" he said, playing the light on the newspaper covering the weapon. "Call come over the radio, said Deputy Dutton, you keep your eyes peeled for this here vehicle."

Behind the sheriff's head, coming from the tower, Ted could see a light bouncing along the road. A running man was almost to the highway. "If there's nothing else, guess I'll be getting on home," Ted said, trying to sound casual.

"Yeah, know what-cha mean. My old woman is always bitching if I come in late." He didn't move away from the car, his light back in Ted's face. "Yesterday I said, Avis, stop your damned bitching, I'll come when I'm damned good and ready."

Ted smiled politely. "Well. I better be going, sheriff."

"When I spotted this here vehicle sitting over yonder, real suspicious like, I figured it was that-un doing all that motorizin'."

"Wasn't this-un, Sheriff. Ain't no crime in parking here, are they?" Behind the constable's back, the man holding the flashlight stepped out on the highway. He waved his hands at passing traffic, trying to flag down a motorist.

"Guess not," Deputy Dutton said, his heavy belly rubbing against Matilda's side mirror. "Them fellows in that black limo you got out of, was looking for it too."

"Must be another-un," Ted said, starting the motor, "a lot of 'em around." Fifty yards away, the man with the flashlight turned and hurried toward the gas station.

The expression on Deputy Dutton's face took on a confidential look, as he stepped away from Matilda. "Well, y'all keep the speed down now, you hear?"

Ted looked serious and waved as Matilda moved slowly by. "I promise. No fast motorizin." He drove past the man holding the flashlight then picked up speed. Through the rear mirror Ted watched him as he stopped and turned back toward Matilda. "They don't give up," he said, smiling. "Good thing we're motorizin' right along, know what I mean, Matilda?"

CHAPTER ELEVEN

The next morning, Betty Ann began preparing breakfast.

Walpole walked in. "Good morning," she said.

"I feel like such a sap. Should of known dem guys couldn't be trusted. Day said there was hard cash in it for me, but day was just stringing me along."

"You must learn to be more circumspect. Remember that part in the Bible that says 'Do unto others and that sort of thing.'"

"Guess I tought I could do unto dem before day done unto me."

Betty Ann giggled. "Goodness, you're incorrigible."

"I needed da money, see?"

"Now, what would you do, if you had all that money?"

"Spend it on my kids. Got five of 'em."

"Mercy, that's a large family."

"Yeah. Their mother died wit da last one." Pain showed in his face. "Now they're livin' wit my sister in Atlanta."

"You poor thing, left with five children to raise."

"Don't get to see 'em too much."

"You poor man."

"Poor? You got dat right, lady. I'm so broke I owe everybody but da Pope. When dem creditors catch up to me, day're gonna nail my aa uh I mean hide to da wall."

"Well, I guess it goes without saying you can't risk telling those men where you're staying now."

"Don't worry, lady. It's my ass on the line too." Realizing that he had used a vulgarity, he winced. "Sheesh I'm sorry."

"You should be, but I'll forgive it this time." She shook her finger in his face good-naturedly. "But don't let it happen again, or I'll tell Ted."

"Dat's swell of you, lady," he said, as Ted walked in.

"What's swell." Ted asked, as he sat down at the kitchen table.

"Mr. Walpole and I were discussing him not revealing his new location to anyone."

"Wise move," Ted said, eyeing Walpole distrustfully.

"Hey, I ain't gonna do dat no more. They're after my aa .. aa .. uh, me too, you know." He glanced nervously at Betty Ann. Her eyebrows were raised, but her expression showed amusement.

"Mr. Wickersham didn't come back, Ted. Wonder what could have happened to that sweet old man?"

"Found somebody new to mooch on, most likely." Betty Ann scowled at him. "He'll show up when they throw him out."

Just then Mark stumbled in, wiping sleep from his eyes. "That bacon smells good."

"There's coffee too," Walpole said, beaming at Betty Ann. "Smells like heaven, don't it."

Mark took a seat on the opposite side of the table from Ted. "Oh! Last night, before I went to bed, I checked my e-mail. There was a message from Dragonfly. He finished decoding most of those names. Said I'd be surprised at one in particular."

"Who's that?"

"Wouldn't say. Wants me to meet with him."

Betty Ann's eyebrows raised. "You've never met him in person?"

"No. only in a chat room."

"Where does he live?"

"I don't know, Betty Ann." She set a platter of bacon and eggs on the table. He took a shred of bacon off the plate and tasted it. "I've been on line with him, on and off, for at least three weeks now. He's okay."

"He could be in Maine, for all you know."

"No. Last night he gave me an address where we could meet, a place in Charlotte on South Boulevard." Mark helped himself to scrambled eggs and bacon, then looked confidently back at Betty Ann. "When I get those names, I'll have the evidence to give the IRS. They'll be too busy with them to bother with me."

Betty Ann placed her hand on his arm. "Couldn't he just mail you the names?"

"I asked him that. Says he needs to talk and he wants me to bring the disk."

"The disk! Is that wise?"

"Part of what I sent on the net got messed up or something."

Ted frowned. "Could be a trap, Mark."

"He's just a harmless hacker, Ted. Besides, I'm dying to see what he looks like."

"How will you get all the way up to Charlotte, Mark? That's an hour's drive from here."

"I've been thinking about that, Betty Ann. Sometimes there's a reward when it's information that the feds really need. I'll split it with you and Ted if I can borrow your car."

"Don't get your hopes up for any reward money, Mark," Betty Ann said, glancing at Ted. "But if it's okay with Ted, you can take Matilda. What do you think, Ted? You can go along and keep an eye on him."

Ted grinned. "Yeah, and I'll take Walpole and the Uzi."

Walpole rolled his eyes at Ted "Relax, you're staying here."

Mark glanced at Betty Ann. "Two of us can handle any little old dragonfly."

CHAPTER TWELVE

Ted stepped out of Matilda onto a dusty gravel parking lot. Mark kept close behind him. The run-down singlewide house trailer, converted to commercial use, sat a scant twenty feet from rushing South Boulevard traffic. Shutters, framing two small front windows, matched the faded green paint on the large weather worn sign perched on the small roof. Dwarfing the building, it proclaimed: "INSURANCE - CHEAP."

"That'll be the day," Ted muttered, as he stepped up onto the small porch. Mark followed him through the front door. The pungent odor of cigarette smoke hit them immediately.

Mark looked around the small office. "No one's here, Ted."

From somewhere in the back, a dog barked and a male voice yelled, "Shut-up, Samson!"

Three steps into the smoky haze, a chest high counter blocked their way. Off to their left, at the end of a hallway through an open door, Mark could see part of an unmade bed and a glowing computer screen. He leaned past an overflowing ashtray on the counter and called out, "Hello?" There was no answer. Then Ted spotted a rusty lobby bell on the counter and tapped it. It clanked dully.

A voice in the back called out, "Hazel, you got customer." They waited, but Hazel didn't show.

Abruptly, a door he hadn't noticed before opened and he could hear the flushing sound of a commode. A woman stepped out into the hallway. She was short, maybe five feet tall and walked toward them with a slight limp. Her hair hung down around her face in a schoolgirl style, but she was definitely no schoolgirl. Mark shuddered at the sight of her watery blue eyes. "Are you the proprietor?" he asked.

A double dose of Max Factor clung to her pudgy face like frosting on a month old wedding cake. In a syrupy sweet voice, she said, "Yeah, darling. Who wants to know?"

"We came to ... ," Mark said. Suddenly he was cut off by the loud ringing of a phone hanging on the wall.

She raised her hand to silence him while picking up a smoldering stub from the crowded ashtray. Turning her back, she lifted the receiver and mumbled into it. Rapid finger movement against the wall punctuated her one-sided conversation. "Uh-huh ... yeah ... guess I could." Expelling acrid fumes through her nose, she unexpectedly yelled, "Same to you, Buddy." Slamming the phone down on its hook, she turned back toward Mark. "Now tell me again, Darling," she said sweetly.

"I was told to meet someone here."

She looked Mark up and down. "Don't get many in here as young as you, sugar. Which was it, DWI or speedin'?"

Mark reddened. "I'm not here to buy auto insurance."

A sarcastic grin added to the lines in her face. "Well you probably couldn't get it anyway. How old are you?"

"That's not why he's here," Ted growled. "Get it over with, Mark."

Callous eyes turned toward Ted. "Who are you, his keeper?"

"If I have to be," Ted said, glaring back at her. "Let the kid talk."

Just then they heard the wailing sound of a siren. Ted froze, then looked out through the smudged front window as a fire truck pulled into the parking lot.

"Harry, come out here," the old crone yelled. "There's a fire truck!" A gaunt deputy old man wearing ragged cut-off bib overalls and beach flip-flops came shuffling down the hall toward them. "And there's smoke!" Hazel said.

Harry wheezed and squinted at her through the haze. "How could ya tell?"

Taking time to light up a fresh coffin nail, she said, "Watch your mouth, old man." A stream of smoke escaped from her nostrils. "The fire, Harry, go see."

"Where's it at?" he said through a mouth, missing teeth.

"My God, Harry, why don't you ask that red-neck on the truck; maybe he'll know something ... get the hell out there!"

Looking like a busted Jack-O-Lantern after the Halloween pranksters ran off, he grinned sheepishly back at her and shuffled out on the porch. He yelled at the fireman unwinding a hose, "Where's it at?"

The firefighter said something under his breath and together they turned and hurried toward the back.

Ignoring the distraction outside, she said in a sugary voice to Mark, "All I sell is insurance, honey."

"I'm supposed to meet someone here, ma'am."

"Who would that be, darling?"

"All I know is his e-mail name."

"E-mail?"

"It's a name you pick to use when you're on line."

"On line?"

"On the Internet ... on the computer."

"Oh," she said, looking puzzled. "Who is it, darlin'?"

"Calls himself Dragonfly."

She snorted, "Kids ... gotta have nifty names, don't-cha."

"He told me to meet him here."

"Well, you can see, there ain't nobody like that around here."

"I'm supposed to give him this disk," Mark said, holding it up. "It's kind of important."

"Well why didn't you say so in the first place." She reached over the counter to take it from his hand.

Quickly, Ted pulled Mark out of her reach. Apologetically, Mark said, "I have to give it to Dragonfly in person."

Her eyes became shrewd. "I'll hold it for him, darling. He'll get it."

"You don't even know what we're talking about," Mark said, becoming angry. "Come on Ted, this must be the wrong address."

"The hell you say!" she said. "That's who was on the phone just now." She took a long drag on her cigarette before continuing.

"Dragonfly said to me, 'Hazel, hold it for me.' I told him I'd be happy to do it."

Ted turned to leave. "Didn't sound happy."

"Wasn't ... 'till he mentioned money."

Ted stopped and looked at Mark. "Money?"

"I didn't say anything about money, honest I didn't, Ted."

"Maybe he smelled it?" Ted muttered, turning back toward Hazel. "What else did he say?"

"When he ask me to get your address, I told him to shove it. I'm not his secretary."

"But, you slammed the phone down," Mark said.

"Yeah. He told me where to go, so I hung up."

A second fire truck pulled into the gravel driveway and parked, blocking Matilda in. Smoke from behind the trailer began to seep through the closed windows. Hazel glanced outside and then rushed to the door. They followed her outside. Making sure she was out of range, Ted said, "You have another copy, don't you?"

"Yeah, and I encrypted this one's."

"Let her have it."

"Why? It's obvious she's lying. She doesn't know Dragonfly."

"Maybe she does," he said. "We'll stake her out."

"Yeah," Mark said. "When Dragonfly comes, we'll follow him."

All of a sudden the old woman came back around the corner of the house, followed by one of the firemen. "Samson," she shrieked, as she dashed into the building through the thick smoke. They were gone for a minute, then she came out again coughing. A big ill-tempered mixed breed rambunctiously pulled them along on his chain.

As the fireman passed, Mark asked, "Is the building burning?"

"Started as a grass fire," he said. "Looks deliberate We'll save the structure, though." He wiped sweat from his eyes. "Kerosene smell all over the place."

"That Howitzer boy, I'll bet," Hazel said. "Just cause I canceled on him last week."

"Somebody went to a lot of trouble," the fireman said. "Kerosene doused everywhere. It started behind the Dumpster."

Hazel's voice sounded grim. "Well, somebody ought to do something about that kid. He lives in the neighborhood."

"We'll look into it, ma'am."

"It had to be him. Yesterday, he told me he'd get even and called me a name." Then she saw Mark and her voice softened. "Why don't you give me that thingamajig, darling. I'll make sure your friend gets it."

"What do you think, Ted?"

Ted looked at Mark and shrugged.

Her hand trembled, as she reached for the disk mark was holding. "I'll make sure he gets it, darlin'. You can count on me."

The aroma of fried chicken, pepper steak and French-fries hung in the air at Mom's Restaurant across the street from the insurance office. Ted and Mark sat in a booth watching through the picture window as the last fire truck pull away. "That took longer than I expected, Ted. It's almost four."

"Uh-huh," he said his mind on something else.

"Shouldn't you call Betty Ann? Let her know what's happening." Mark fished in his pocket for change for the pay phone and handed it to Ted. "I'll keep watch."

Time passed, used supper dishes had been cleared away except for the ones in front of Ted and Mark. After the movie down the street let out, the night crowd wandered in for pie and coffee. Their waitress came over to the table again, this time eyeing them openly. "We close at midnight." Mark looked up at her, his embarrassment showing. Ted ignored her as she stood there like a sentry, not moving. Under his breath, Mark said, "No one's come or gone, Ted."

"Yeah," he growled. "Where's Dragonfly?"

"He wouldn't show up this late, would he?"

Glancing back at the waitress, Ted dropped a tip on the table. She looked surprised, then relieved. "Let's go," he said.

Across the street Hazel stood in a darkened bedroom and stared out at the restaurant. "Look Harry, they're still sitting there, bold as brass. How dumb can they be?"

"What'd you expect from 'em. In the old days, people knew better than to sit in the light to do a stake out."

"Well, Dragonfly sure ain't gonna show up with them sitting in that window like that." Snickering, she turned away. "He could pop both of 'em for sure, if he wanted to."

"Why would Dragonfly want to do that?"

"Don't know, just thinking out loud." She lit a new cigarette from the burning ember of the one in her hand. "If they get too close, I guess. They're finally leaving."

CHAPTER THIRTEEN

The next morning Mark booted up the computer. A few minutes later he ran down the hall, calling to Ted who was just coming out of the shower, "You won't believe this!" Mark led him into the computer room. "Look for yourself," he said, pointing at the computer screen.

Ted stared at the computer. "You're right," he said. "I don't believe it!"

Betty Ann, hearing the commotion, came in. Reading the message, she said, "What don't you not believe?"

"Read it again," Ted said.

She read it once more. "My goodness, so he had a wreck, what's the big deal?"

"Don't you see?" Mark said. "That's just a lame excuse."

"I've had wrecks before, Mark. They always kept me from showing up somewhere on time."

"You don't understand. If he'd of come there yesterday, we'd have seen him!"

"Maybe he got it early this morning."

"This has yesterday's date," Ted said. "Something's fishy."

"We watched the place the whole day," Mark said, exasperation in his voice. "Like a hawk guarding chickens."

"So?" She still looked puzzled.

"The message says, 'Hazel *gave* me the disk!'" He stared at her. "No one entered the whole time we watched. When did Hazel give it to him?"

"Oh," she said. She reread the message very slowly out loud. "Hazel gave me the disk and I'm working on it. Sorry for the no-show, an auto accident delayed me until after five." She brightened. "He came in through the back door!"

"There wasn't one," Mark said. "It burned, and the firemen boarded it over."

"Well, my goodness." Then a thought came to her. "Get him on our computer again, Mark. Why don't you ask him about it?"

"I'm already on it," he said, sitting back down at the keyboard, he started to type.

Just then Walpole stuck his head through the door. "What's all da commotion about?"

"Never mind," Ted said, his face looking grave. Pulling him out of the room and walking him down the hall to the kitchen table, he said, "Now, it's your turn."

"My turn! Sheesh, what now?"

"The reason I came to you."

"Oh yeah, I was wondering 'bout dat."

"I heard you have friends"

Suspiciously, Walpole said, "What kind of friends you talkin' about?"

"In high places."

Walpole wiped nervous perspiration from his upper lip. "So?"

"So, I want your friend to run a check for somebody on Interpol."

"Interpol!" His eyes rolled. "Dat's heavy stuff."

"Yeah ... so can he?"

He was silent for a minute. "You mean like if they're lookin' for somebody?"

"Yeah."

Relaxing a bit, Walpole said, "My brother knows a cop in da city. He's at a front desk, know what I mean?"

"So?"

"He could check on da Pope if ya got da right kind of scratch."

"How about escaped war criminals?"

"Sheesh, is dat all?" He relaxed. "What's his name?"

"Matthew Wielding, he was a Sergeant in Germany."

"In da big war?"

"Yeah."

"You want his rap sheet, right?"

"No," Ted said, his face a mask. "Not that."

"Den what are we talkin' 'bout here?"

"If he's still on the list."

Walpole's eyes became shrouded and suspicious. "What list would dat be?"

"Are they still looking for him!"
"Oh." He relaxed again.
"Don't let on who's asking."
"Hey, I wasn't born yesterday you know."
"And this is just between you and me."
"Dat's cool. Who is dis guy, anyway?"
"He disappeared."
"I figured dat. What's he to you?"
"You ask too many questions."
"Hey, I gotta know if I'm getting into something too deep."
"He owes me money."
"Oh, is dat it."
"How soon will you know? I'm in a hurry."
"If I can phone from here, real soon."
Casually, Ted asked, "What's the tab gonna be?"
"Not too steep."
"I'm kind of broke."
"Hey, don't worry 'bout it, we can work somethin' out."
"Then do it now."

Walpole huddled with the phone to his ear and his hand cupped over the mouthpiece to prevent Ted from hearing. A short time later he slowly put it back on the cradle. His eyes were bigger than usual when he came back over and sat back down. "You say dis guy owes you money?"

"Yeah."

"Well, he could pay off da national debt if he wanted to. Got enough war loot to live on for two lifetimes, at least."

"What about the wanted list?"

"At da very top. He stole a pot full of diamonds. Must be worth millions in today's market." Walpole couldn't contain his excitement. "Some of dem was registered, you know what I mean? Just like race horses and show dogs, day got identification papers."

"How can they tell?"

"It's all on their inventory report."

"Not that."

"What?"

"One diamond from another?"

"Some of 'em has flaws or funny shapes, stuff like dat. Day describe all dat kinda stuff on da paper when day register 'em."

"So?"

"The box dat he stole had a lot of dat kind in it. Some of dem rocks was real famous. You know Krauts kept records of everyting day stole. Made it easy for da brass to know what was missing."

"So, where are they looking?"

"In jewelry stores and museums, I guess."

"No, for him."

"Yeah, I wanted to know dat too," Walpole said, greedy eyes shifting back and forth. "He might still have a few left lying around, know what I mean?" His words ran together as he continued, "He's here in da states somewhere. Day found one of da biggest rocks in Hong Kong a while back. Den one showed up in South America someplace and last year one popped up in Atlanta."

Ted blanched. "So they *are* looking for him over here."

Walpole wiped nervous perspiration from his forehead. "And he's still got a pot full."

"What makes you think that?"

"At least no more has cropped up." Walpole looked shrewdly at Ted. "Tink you'd recognize him now after all these years?"

"I might. Why?"

"There's a reward out. Gives us an edge, don't you tink?"

"What do you mean?"

"We got two shots at da brass ring dis time out. He could give us a handful not to turn him in, or we could turn him over for da reward. Either way, we get stinkin' rich."

"Forget it."

"Sheesh, don't ya like money?"

Just then Betty Ann walked in. Overhearing the end of their conversation, she said curiously, "Who doesn't like money?" Ted looked sternly at Walpole and he shut up. "What are you two talking about so seriously?"

"Just man talk," he said, glaring at Walpole who remained silent. "What about Dragonfly?"

"All he'd say is that he's working on it," Betty Ann said. "Mark didn't tell him we knew he didn't come back last night."

Ted looked grimily at Betty Ann. "Remember that guy I told you about?"

"Who, darling?"

He signaled her with his eyes. She recognized the look to pay close attention. "That owed me money?"

"Oh." Her eyebrows shot up. "What about him?"

Controlling his voice, he said, "He's in the states now."

"How did you find that out?"

Nodding at Walpole, he said, "He made a call."

"Well good for you, Mr. Walpole," Betty Ann said, forcing a smile, "Where do they think he is?"

"If I knew dat, I'd be looking for him too. He's got a frig ... uh ... a bunch of loot I hear."

"Well, you'd better stay as far away from that man as you can." She glanced at Ted and grinned impishly. "Ted told me he could be mighty dangerous."

"Day tink he's in Atlanta," Walpole said, beginning to pace the floor. "My family's there, you know. We could all crash at my sister's house; give Ted a chance to keep a look out for him." His eyes pleaded with them. "Since Ted knows what he looks like and all."

Betty Ann held back a laugh. "Why, that's mighty kind of you, Mr. Walpole. What do you think, Ted?"

"I'll let you know." Ted's eyes met Betty Ann's. "If they don't find him first."

"Well, all you really wanted to know was if that old boy was still alive and around somewhere. Now you know for sure, darlin'."

"Yeah," he said, looking grim. "Now I know."

Suddenly, the phone rang. Betty Ann picked it up. "Hello?" Five seconds went by before she put her hand over the receiver and whispered, "Its Mr. Wickersham!" After a short conversation she said, "We certainly will Mr. Wickersham. You take care now." Then she hung up.

"Well?" Ted growled. "What's his story?"

"He apologized for not calling sooner, but he just now found our phone number."

"It's in the book." Ted looked skeptical. "Took him long enough."

"He couldn't remember your last name at first."

"Where was he calling from?"

"Didn't say. That's funny, he didn't leave a number where he could be reached, either." Betty Ann blanched. "Oh Ted, I hope he's not in the clutches of those thugs." She looked at Ted, the question hanging in the air. "He did say not to worry ... and would we please hold his belongings for a day or so until he can retrieve them."

"If doze guys has him," Walpole said, "day'll show up here real soon."

Betty Ann shivered. "Oh, thank you, Mr. Walpole for that comforting thought."

"Hey, lady. I always say, it's better to jump before da ship hits da sand, know what I mean?" He glanced uneasily at Ted. "You know, read da music before da band director wiggles his thing-a-ma-jig."

Betty Ann repressed a giggle. "Well what do you suggest we do, then?"

"Get out of here fast. Go to Atlanta."

"Should have known you'd say that, Mr. Walpole. You want to find that soldier and get your hands on those diamonds."

"What's wrong wit dat? Don't you want to be rich?"

"You're incorrigible, Mr. Walpole! Those diamonds are long gone. That took place years ago."

"Well day hasn't showed up yet, has day? You'd tink day would of by now."

"Forget about the diamonds." She turned toward Ted. "What about that big car sitting out back?"

"What about it?"

"We can't just leave it back there."

"I'll get rid of it."

"What will you do, Ted?" Betty Ann glanced nervously through the front window again. "You can't bury it."

"Drive it to Charlotte."

"You mean just leave it on the street someplace?"

Mark came in, overhearing the conversation, he said, "Why not leave it at the Airport. They'll think you took a plane someplace."

Betty Ann's face lit up. "That's a good idea, Mark. And we can rent a car there. One the mob won't recognize."

"Just in case I'll take along the Uzi."

CHAPTER FOURTEEN

Ted withdrew a ticket from the slot and the gate opened to the long term parking lot. Leaving the ticket on the dashboard, they exited the limo and waited for the shuttle. "What about the key?" Betty Ann asked. "You know you didn't lock the car."

"It's in the limo." Ted looked amused. "Maybe someone will steal it."

Betty Ann giggled. "That would throw 'em off, wouldn't it!"

A shuttle pulled up and they entered the empty bus. "Where to?" the driver asked.

"United Airlines."

Ten minutes later, the bus stopped in front of a row of skycaps working feverishly processing bags. Entering the building, they blended in with the crowd of travelers, and descended the escalator to the baggage claim area. People jostled and pushed as they retrieved luggage gliding by on the circular conveyor belts.

"Hertz is over yonder someplace," Betty Ann said, pointing at a line of rental booths on the far side of the room. Suddenly, she grabbed Ted's arm. "Ted, it's him!"

"Who?" he said starting to turn in the direction that she was looking.

"Don't look.'" She pulling him behind a family waiting for their luggage. "One of the goons from the tower!"

"You sure?"

"I'll never forget that face, Ted. He was in the limo when they took us to the tower." Ted looked in time to see the man that he had observed running toward him at the gas station. He was leaving through a sliding glass door, carrying two suitcases. Keeping people between them, Ted and Betty Ann followed and watched from a distance as he sat them down beside a large Jeep double-parked at the curb. A tall figure, with his back to Ted, bent over and checked the bags carefully, then nodded to his chauffeur who lifted them into the back. As the Grand Wagoner drove by, the tall man glanced past Betty Ann.

"Ted, he was at the tower also." Her words running together excitedly, she said, "He was the one ordering them around up there. He tried to stay hidden, but I got a good look at him when he came out of the shadows once. He must be the big boss, Ted!" Betty Ann shivered. "His eyes were as blue as the sky. Mercy, he frightens me."

Their rental car, a large white Chevrolet, moved quietly through the Charlotte streets. Betty Ann giggled. "Are you going to take Walpole up on his Atlanta trip?"

"You kidding?" The big car passed under a yellow light and Ted quickly glanced in the rear mirror in time to see it turn red. "What's the point?"

"Yeah, the little ninny doesn't know he'd be looking for someone he's already found." She giggled again. "Thought I'd choke, when he asked you, if you thought you'd recognize the sergeant after all these years."

"Bet I'd know the General."

"He's probably living it up somewhere in Hong Kong. Sold the diamonds and getting fat from all that greasy food."

"Yeah? Then what about Atlanta?"

"You mean who sold that one?" She looked puzzled. "Could have been anybody. Maybe someone bought one from him down there, then smuggled it up here to sell."

"Glad I didn't sell my last two." They sped down highway 74 past Sweet Union Flea Market. "Cut like teardrops."

"A pair like that are bound to be on that list. You were smart," she said. "Besides, someday, you can make me a set of ear rings out of 'em."

"Wear 'em to the grocery store?"

"I wouldn't *wear* them," she said dreamily. "Just sit at home and hold them in my hand. Then when this has all blown over, we'll sell 'em and really be rich."

"No," Ted said stoically. "That'd be big trouble."

"You were lucky you made it out of Venezuela with all that money taped to your bellybutton."

"Customs thought I was just fat."

Betty Ann put a sympathetic hand on his knee. "That took a lot of nerve smuggling all that money in past New Orleans customs."

"Too young to know better. Must have been a thousand soldiers coming through that day."

Betty Ann smiled. "And you were desperate enough to try anything."

"Money's kept me from getting caught all these years." He glanced at her and smiled. "You've lived okay, haven't you?"

"Like a queen, lover, like a queen." She smiled again. "With you working those construction jobs, you've never needed a social security number. Its worked out pretty good all the way round."

"So far, Doll. So far."

As they drove past the silo Ted became silent. Finally he said, "The man with the blue eyes?"

"At the airport?"

Nodding, he said, "There's something about him."

"What do you mean?"

"Don't know," he said darkly. "It bugs me."

CHAPTER FIFTEEN

Chimes down the street at the college for the morning classes struck ten just as Deputy Dutton stepped up on the front porch. Breathing heavily from the exertion, the heavyset man pushed the doorbell button several times in quick succession. Betty Ann, startled by the sudden noise, ran to the window and peeked through the thin curtains. "It's a policeman, Ted," she whispered. "Hide!"

Slipping from the living room, he stood around the corner in the hallway. "Careful what you say, Doll."

She opened the door and in a pleasant southern voice said, "Good morning officer."

"Morning, Ma'am." Politely he removed his smoky-the-bear hat and wiped sweat from his forehead with a damp handkerchief. "Name's Dutton, Deputy Dutton, ma'am." Betty Ann watched patiently while he mopped the cap's headband. He looked up and smiled self-consciously. "Already hot, ain't it." His walleye stared past her into the living room.

She remained in the doorway behind the locked screen. "Is there something wrong?"

"Naw, I just has to ask some questions." He smiled good-naturedly. "Been going to all these here houses around here, know what I mean?"

She unhooked the screen door and stepped out onto the front porch. "I wondered when y'all would get around to it."

He looked suspiciously down at her. "What's that, Ma'am?"

"The fire?"

He tucked his chin into his chest and grinned. "How'd y'all know?"

"Well, my goodness, what else could it be? That's the biggest thing that's happened in this old neighborhood in at least a fortnight."

"Yes'um," he said, looking sheepish. Then his expression became solemn. "Y'all see anything suspicious like?"

Betty Ann hesitated, as she turned the question over in her mind. "Why yes I did, come to think about it." Wiping her hands, drying them on her apron, her expression became serious. "There was a big old black hearse looking car that passed by several times. Who ever was in it sure was interested in that house on fire." She began to warm to the discussion. "The windows were as black as the ace of spades. No way a person could see inside. Now that was suspicious, don't you think?"

"Yes'um."

She placed her hand on his arm, a confidential look on her face. "Tell me sheriff, what do you think made that old house burn up that way?"

"Natural gas explosion, most likely, ma'am. Gas lines is always accidentin' like that. Somebody must of left a jet turned on. It accidented that old house all to hell."

Feigning astonishment, she covered her mouth with her hand. "You don't say? Somebody could have gotten themselves killed!"

"Yes'um. Weren't nobody to home, best we can figure out." His head turned and his walleye wandered off across the street toward the part of the blackened building that was still standing. "Course them in Monroe said it looked more like it was set, but who'd want to do such a thing as that?"

"You can never tell, sheriff. There's a lot of mean people in this old world."

"Yes'um, know what you mean. Somebody got his self pushed off the top of that old silo out on the edge of town, just the other day."

"Mercy me," she said looking shocked. Her voice trailed off. "Well I never!"

"Yes'um. Who ever done it, pushed another great big ol' guy down a elevator shaft that same night."

"My goodness! What's this would coming to?"

"Yes'um."

"If you catch up to that big black car, I'll bet you'll find out who set that fire." Eyes squinting, her face took on a determined look. "When it drove by they sure were interested in it."

"Couldn't of been none of them in that limo, ma'am. I already talked to them folks." He looked down at his feet and shook his head knowingly. "They was looking for some feller by the name of Matthew J. Wielding."

"Oh?" she said, hiding her surprise. Casually she continued, "Did they find him?"

"No ma'am. Ain't nobody living in the county by that name, leastwise not listed in no telephone book nor on any of them tax records." Suddenly, he stood taller with a self-important expression on his face. "I know that for sure, cause he paid me a hundred dollar bill just to look it up for him on the tax books."

"What in the world does he want with that Wielding person?"

"Didn't say for sure, but that big blue eyed man in the limo is willing to pay me another hundred if I ever run across him."

"That much?"

"Yes'um. That Wielding feller must owe him a lot of money and I could tell that he surly aims to get it back."

"Well, I'll let you know if I ever hear tell of him," Betty Ann said. "Maybe you'll split the reward?"

"He ain't around here, ma'am," he said hastily, "but thanks for the kind offer." Deputy Dutton quickly stepped off the porch and put his cap back on his balding head. "Don't you worry your pretty head none, ma'am. If he shows up around here, I'll nab him real quick like. You take care now, you hear?"

CHAPTER SIXTEEN

Betty Ann shut the door and turned around in time to see Walpole and Mark standing beside Ted. She giggled, hiding the apprehension she felt. "Could you hear, Ted? Don't think he wants to split any reward money."

"Did he say Wielding?"

Guarding her expression from the others, she nodded, her eyes becoming grave. "Why in the world would that person in the limousine want him, Ted?"

"Day must of heard about da diamonds!" Walpole said. "Maybe dem hoods will leave us alone now."

"Why is that, Mr. Walpole?" Betty Ann said. "Nothing's changed, as far as I can see."

"Foxes won't chase squirrels when there's a hen on da nest."

"What on earth does that mean?"

Mark butted in, "Betty Ann, he means chickens are slower and easier to catch."

Walpole smiled slyly at her. "Wielding has da diamonds; we don't; day'll go after him like bees after honey."

Betty Ann stomped her foot looking aggravated. "You boys are fooling yourselves. This is not the end of it. Two of their people were killed! Don't forget that?"

"She's right." Ted said, "Won't let that pass."

Walpole rolled his eyes. "We gotta get out of town, den!"

"You mean Atlanta, Mr. Walpole?" Alarm suddenly replaced by amusement, she said, "You only have one thing on your mind, don't you."

His voice trailing off he said lamely, "Day won't be lookin' for us there!"

"Speaking of people dying, listen to what I just found out," Mark said. "I searched the name Felix Fluggy on the NET and it showed up in an article in a New York paper two weeks ago."

"So? Who's Felix Fluggy?"

"The name Dragonfly decoded, remember, Ted?"

"Oh yeah."

"Well, he's dead."

"So?"

"Here's the interesting part. He was killed by government agents near Waxhaw, North Carolina."

Betty Ann's eyebrows shot up. "That's near here!"

"Isn't that a little coincidental?" Mark said. "Think about it!"

"What kind of coincidental you talkin' 'bout here?" Walpole asked. "Good coincidental or da bad kind?"

Mark caught the sneer on his face, and blushed crimson. "People that are after us and a guy that I found on their files ended up here in our little county? That's a real coincidence, don't you think?"

Walpole snickered and looked away. "Sheesh, so what?"

Undaunted, Mark continued. "The story said that a shoot-out took place near Wingate. He was hit but managed to escape. FBI agents picked up his trail in Monroe, near the courthouse and caught up with him again twelve miles down the road on the railroad tracks near Waxhaw." Mark hesitated, looking intently from Betty Ann to Ted to Walpole, savoring their various expressions. "But the second shoot-out killed him." Triumphantly he announced, "And the contraband he was carrying was never found."

Walpole suddenly became interested. "Contraband?"

"Diamonds!" Mark said, watching him wipe drool from his lips as his words sunk in. "The story said he was a suspected mule for the mob. The FBI had been following him, hoping he would lead them to the top man."

Ted grunted and glanced at Betty Ann.

Walpole's eye began to twitch. "How many diamonds we talkin' 'bout here?"

Mark grinned, his young face beaming. "Thought that'd get your attention."

"When did this happen?"

"About five years ago, Betty Ann."

"No, that couldn't be. We would have heard about it," she said. "It would have been in all the papers around here."

"Happened in the dead of night, out in the country." Mark looked back at Ted. "Guess the local news never heard about it. The FBI is very secretive."

Walpole licked his lips. "So how come?"

"How come what?"

"You know, how come a New York paper was da only one to publish dat five year old story?"

"Maybe the FBI released it to 'em on purpose. Did you ever think of that?"

Betty Ann smiled. "Now Mark, you're letting your imagination run away with you. Why would they do such a thing?"

"To flush out the head man, Betty Ann. If he finally learned what happened to his mule, wouldn't he want to come looking for his loot?"

Walpole's eyes glittered. "Ya never said how many rocks there was."

"A bag full, the paper said.

"Tink day might be 'round here someplace, Mark?"

Mark grinned jubilantly. "If I were that mob chief, I'd sure be looking, or I'd be sending somebody." He lifted both hands palm up. "Hello? Couldn't it be that's why that gang is here now?"

Walpole's whiny voice trembled, "Yeah, dat could be it. Flatfoot Fluggy dropped it off somewheres before day caught up to him. If da feds ain't found it yet," his voice trailed off and he licked his lips, "da bag's still gotta be around here someplace."

"And so are those bad people," Betty Ann said. "Don't forget that, Mr. Walpole"

His eyes clouded over. "Are we talking about dem same diamonds here?"

"According to the story," Mark said, "he was carrying a bag full."

"How big a bag, do ya tink?"

"They said it was a Bull Durham sack. How big is that?"

"Tobacco used to come in dem little cloth bags," Walpole said gleefully, "back den people rolled their own." His eyes grew even larger. "Small enough to fit in your shirt pocket." He licked his lips greedily. "Bag dat size could hold thirty maybe forty diamonds. Dat's a lot of loot!"

"Or a lot of trouble," Betty Ann cautioned.

He looked from Betty Ann to Ted to Mark. "Maybe we should stay here after all. Take a look around. Say near da tracks in Waxhaw or maybe da train station in Monroe."

"My goodness, Mr. Walpole, that happened five years ago. Don't you think somebody's already done that?"

"I got a nose for these kind of tings, lady. Day can't have looked everywhere. If day had, da merchandize would of already been found and we'd of heard about it already."

"Better think it over," Mark said. "She's right. The mob is out there too."

Betty Ann suddenly took Ted by the hand and led him down the hallway to their bedroom, leaving the two men in a heated conversation. Inside the bedroom, with the door closed, she said, "That man in the limo is looking for *you*, Ted! Why?"

"Yeah, why?"

"Right here in Union County, they're looking for Sergeant Wielding!" Ted's dark eyebrows knitted. Betty Ann had never seen him so disquieted before. "Someone in the mob must have run across the Air Force court-martial papers."

"And they think I still have 'em."

"How did they trace you this far?" Tears came to her eyes. "No wonder the mob's after you!"

"Only have two."

"We have to figure this out, Ted. You sold one to that ship's captain that smuggled you to Caracas and the big one to the pawn shop when you got into port."

"That was two of my four."

"They think you have them all. What are we going to do?"

"General kept 'em." He studied the floor.

"That happened a long time ago, Ted. Nothing in Venezuela connects you to here, does it?"

"Heard a man down there got caught."

"You told me. A week after he gave you all that money and *that* diamond turned out to be famous."

"Worth a lot more than he paid me. It belonged to a king or something from Salzburg."

"That's in Austria, isn't it?" He nodded. "The General gave you those because he knew they'd be recognized hoping you'd be caught or shot." Ted stared at the floor looking grim. "Almost figured that out too late."

"Lucky you got out of Caracas before that pawnbroker was caught. He must have told people about you."

"He thought I was a German."

"You never told him you were American?"

He shook his head. "Said I was headed for Bolivia." Looking shrewdly at Betty Ann, he said, "Germans hid out there after the war."

"But the pawnbroker saw you, Ted. There would have been a wanted poster with your picture on it. He'd recognize you from that." She sat on the bed beside him a consoling hand on his knee. "That's why they're looking for you *here*. They guessed that you came back to the states."

"Yeah, could be."

"Oh, Ted, now the mob is after you just like the military." She looked sadly into his eyes. "Could that Bull Durham sack be part of those same diamonds in the footlocker?"

"Don't know."

"If they are, the General must have hired that Corsair Enterprises Company to smuggle 'em over here!"

"Or sold 'em the whole trunk full," he said grimly.

"My goodness, that thing with that Flatfoot person all happened over five years ago, Ted. You think they really didn't know what happened to him 'till the story was leaked?"

"Looks like it."

"They'll do anything to get their diamonds back."

Remembering the house exploding across the street, he said, "But they must know I don't have 'em. If they thought I did, they wouldn't dare torch the house. They'd loose 'em."

Betty Ann sat quietly for a minute then her face brightened. "Wouldn't our house guests be surprised to find out you are the Sergeant Wielding they're all looking for?" Ted didn't smile. "And that the General sold all those diamonds to the mob."

"Uh-huh. But why is the don looking for me, then?" Ted looked grimly into Betty Ann's upturned face. "Think we saw him."

"You think that tall person at the airport with the blue eyes is the don?"

"Uh-huh." Ted's face remained somber. "There's something familiar about him."

"He *was* the one in charge at the tower. They sure jumped when he spoke."

"Seen him before," Ted said. "Can't remember where."

"If he's the don, the FBI would love to know about him." She looked into his eyes, searching for clues to his thoughts. "Are you going to tell them?"

"You know I can't."

"Well, maybe I could." She was quiet for a minute thinking about it. "It could keep 'em off your back."

"You don't know that. Keep out of it," he said, his voice trailing off. "And stay hidden if we can."

When they came back, Walpole was on the phone. Receiver cradled in the crook of his neck, his free hand waving in the air. "So that's all you know, Little Brother?" he yelled. "I could of tole ya dat much! Tanks for nothin'!" Slamming the phone down, he turned back toward Mark. "Day picked up da mule's trail near dat courthouse in Monroe. Chased him to where he jumped in a freight car and got away. Day was waiting for da train near Waxhaw and stopped it." Coming over to the kitchen table, he sat down and studied the tabletop sullenly. Then he looked up. "When he made da run for it, day plugged him again; dis time he wasn't so lucky."

"That's all?" Betty Ann said. "That's not much to go on."

"My little brother said day asked Flatfoot about da bag he was carryin' before he croaked; and all he said was 'God Rest Our Confederate Soldiers.'"

His nasal whine became shriller. "Main ting is, he didn't have da merchandise on him so he must of stashed it somewheres along da tracks. Dat's where I'm looking first."

Betty Ann scowled, "There's over twelve miles between Monroe and Waxhaw. You planning to walk all of it?"

He grinned back at her. "Does a beer-can have a sucky-hole?" Enthusiastically he continued, "If you guys won't take me to Monroe, I'll call a cab or stick out my thumb. Get there any way I can."

"You know that happened years ago. You don't have ..."

He held up his hand, interrupting her as he headed for the door. "Nobody's talking me out of dis, lady. Saw a bus stop by dat Klondike beanery. I'm catching it now."

Ted glanced knowingly toward Betty Ann before he spoke. "Wasting your time."

Walpole caught the smug look that passed between them and his face turned red. "Well it ain't showed up yet, has it? If it's still out there, I'm gonna find it!"

Betty Ann giggled, "Go ahead, look all you want, but you better be careful. There could be all kinds of snakes out there." Hiding her amusement, she said, "Some even crawling on the ground." He blanched and she snickered again. "Remember, I told you so."

"Tanks," he sneered. "Wait and see who's laughin' when I show up back here wit da stash in my hand." Stepping onto the front porch, he stopped and turned. "I'm gonna be rich, lady; you'll see, day'll all see."

Ted walked to the curtain and watched him as he limped swiftly out of sight. "You trust him, Doll?"

"If you mean will he go back to the mob? He's learned his lesson with that nest of vipers, Ted." She wiped tears from her eyes. "Besides, his little mind is so full of avarice, he won't think of anything else for a while."

"Won't find 'em."

"Maybe he will. But if he doesn't, at least he'll not be looking for Sergeant Wielding." Ted shot her a warning look. She blushed and glanced at Mark who was listening with an interested expression on his face.

"No one knows what he looks like, Betty Ann. Could be he's dead."

"That's right, Mark." Quickly she changed the subject. "Maybe Dragonfly has decoded some more names. I'd give a penny to know more about that tall blue eyed man. If he's the don, he must be on the list." As Mark walked back down the hall toward the computer room, Betty Ann whispered, "Does he suspect?"

"Maybe."

"You know Walpole really could find that little old sack. He sure is determined."

"Yeah," Ted said sarcastically.

Suddenly, Mark came back down the hall, exasperation written across his young face. "Dragonfly's done it!"

"What now?"

"He knows about Fluggy, Betty Ann, that's what! He e-mailed me again! He's found out about Flatfoot." He saw the question on her face. "Same way I did. Surfing the net."

Betty Ann's eyebrows raised. "Then he knows about the bag of diamonds?"

Mark nodded, frustration showing in his eyes. "Told me if I find 'em first, he wants half for giving me the information."

"Then he thinks you'll be looking?"

Mark nodded. "I told him, the same goes for him. If he finds 'em, I get half. He agreed."

"Wouldn't it be fun to be a little bird out there." She grinned at them impishly. "I mean watching him and Mr. Walpole along the tracks dodging the FBI and the mob, falling all over each other looking for that little old needle in a haystack?"

Suddenly, Mark's face lit up. "Don't think we can lose on this one. If Dragonfly finds the bag, we get half." Suddenly he turned to Ted. "We still don't know who he is, or even what he looks like. That could be a real disadvantage."

Betty Ann put a consoling hand on his arm. "If he should happen to find the bag, Mark, you'll never know it."

"Now Betty Ann, we have to start trusting people sometime."

"Oh Mark, you are so young, so innocent."

CHAPTER SEVENTEEN

On the Haynes Street overpass in Monroe, Walpole glanced around, making sure that he had not been followed. Leaning over the cement railing, he looked down at the ancient station house a hundred feet below. An old black man leisurely swept the dusty concrete porch nestled close against the triple set of railroad tracks. Farther out in the bright sunlight, a tramp carrying a bulging burlap bag, trudged along the gleaming rails. A floppy hat pulled down to his eyebrows covered his head, as he stopped and picked up an object from the tall grass beside the tracks. He inspected it for a second. Then dropping it into his pocket, he continued along the rails.

Movement caught Walpole's attention when suddenly the janitor dropped his broom and hunched over a small device he held close to his mouth. In a parking lot a hundred yards away, two men stepped from a parked mini-van and ran toward the tramp. He saw them at once. Dropping the sack, he sprinted across the three sets of tracks and dodged behind a parked freight car. A silencer muffled the sound, but Walpole saw the flash from the pursuer's pistol and heard the smack of a bullet hitting metal siding.

Startled into action, Walpole began to quickly retrace his steps back across the bridge. He rushed along watching the two men as they reached the boxcar with pistols drawn. They eased around the corner and out of his view. Two quick shots rang out. Walpole ducked instinctively.

"That ain't no silencer!" he muttered as he reached the curb. Trying to look invisible, he hurried up Haynes Street toward the safety of the courthouse. Suddenly, a car came out of nowhere and pulled up beside him. Still rolling, the door opened and, too late, he recognized the thug in the limo. He was dragged inside and the car picked up speed.

Walpole's face stung from the slap that had encouraged him to enter quickly. He rubbed it nervously. Pinned in the corner, hyperventilating and nauseated with fear, the pungent odor of

Bourbon and stale cigar smoke filled his lungs. He whimpered, "Where you taking me? I ain't done nothin'."

The man's eyes, hard as a marble statue, showed no expression. "Tying up loose ends is all. It's just business."

The mobster behind the steering wheel eyed him coolly through the rearview mirror. "Yeah, loose ends."

Walpole rubbed his face and stared at the pimples on the back of the driver's neck. "I ain't no loose end."

The guy beside him grinned evilly. "You better do like the boss says double-quick."

"He'll do kinky stuff to you," the driver said, snickering."

The car stopped in front of a Knight's Inn motel and the two hoods hustled Walpole out and into a suite of rooms. One stayed with him while the other went to the adjoining room. A few minutes later he returned.

"You know a tall drink of water, calls himself Ted Lowen?"

Walpole thought about it for a second, a nervous tic developing under one eye. "Yeah," he said, trying desperately to control the trembling in his voice. "Came to my office once. Why?"

"Shut up, I'll ask the questions. Where's he live?"

"Sheesh, how would I know dat?"

The unexpected backhand caught Walpole by surprise and the hood growled, "You want some more? Watch your mouth."

The little PI cringed away and put his hand to the new hurt spot. "What da hell's he got to do wit me?" he whimpered. "I only seen him dat once."

"The boss needs him found." More to himself than Walpole he mumbled under his breath. "He iced two of our soldiers today."

"You talking 'bout down on da tracks?"

"Yeah, on the tracks."

"Sheesh, I saw part of dat! Day had dat guy cold." He rubbed his face again. "So dat's what happened!"

"Guess its okay to tell you. You ain't gonna be around to tell nobody."

Walpole's hand wiped a tear from his cheek. "How'd you know it was him? All I saw was dat old bum."

"That's what he wanted you to see. Saw him earlier without his disguise."

"Without his disguise, huh." This new information made Walpole bolder. "What'd he look like wit-out his disguise on?"

"Tall, dark hair, bushy eyebrows."

Walpole stalled for time. "What was he doing down there on da tracks, anyway?"

"Looking for something, same as us. You ask a lot of questions for a dead man walking."

Ignoring the chilling thought, Walpole's mind raced, trying to put the pieces together. *I was with him only an hour ago. He couldn't of got out there that fast!* "Sounds like dat Ted person all right. He must be a good shot, to get da drop on dem two like dat."

"Yeah, they was the best." Dragging him to his feet, he said, "Come on, the boss will see you now."

It was dark in the next room. Only a small gooseneck table lamp on a desk was lit. It pointed out toward Walpole. A man sitting behind the desk was holding a phone to his ear. Unlike the other men, he had the sophisticated appearance of the rich and pampered. In spite of the warm weather, he wore dark blue kid gloves, pinstriped suit and an elegant paisley necktie. His long face, half in shadow, suddenly looked up; piercing blue eyes fixed on Walpole.

Sheesh, da guy from da tower!

Slowly he put the telephone back on the cradle and picked up a dagger from the desktop. The eight-inch blade glittered menacingly. Repeatedly, he thrust the tip into the desk top. From the dark behind the gooseneck lamp, he contemplated the terrified private eye standing before him. His articulate voice, with its clipped New England accent, sounded ominous. "On our last encounter, you were dangling over the side of that silo, like a fat little porker ready to be slaughtered."

Someone in the room stifled a nervous laugh and, without moving his head, he cut his eyes in their direction. The thug backed off a step and ducked his head. Turning the cold blue eyes back on Walpole, he pointed the blade toward him. "What happened up there, porky?"

"Up where?"

Instantly, a hand came out of the dark from behind Walpole and hit him hard across the back of his head. Falling forward, he caught himself on the desk. At once, the mafia soldier stepped closer and held him there. "Show a little respect, ass hole. You're talkin' to the don."

Walpole held on with both hands and shook his head to clear it. "I wasn't too sure where you was talkin' 'bout, dat's all. You must mean on dat old silo."

Quickly, the don stuck the dagger-tip against Walpole's throat. "You took out Francis and Red up there. How'd you do that?"

"I didn't do nothin', I swear! When I climbed back onto da roof, all I seen was dem dead bodies on da floor." Trying to inch away from the blade, he whined, "I heard da elevator comin' back up, so I hid. I swear, dat's all!"

While thinking over what Walpole had said, the don withdrew the knife and began to scratch on a half-finished design on the desk. The soldier released his grip and Walpole relaxed a little. Then he saw the gleaming skull and crossbones on the handle and the swastika engraved on the blade and he began to tremble all over again. "Three of my best men couldn't take out big Francis on their best day. Who helped you?"

"Nobody helped me. I mean, I didn't do nothin', I just hid, dat's all."

"My associates informed me that they searched the roof; you weren't there."

"Well, day didn't look so good, did day." The hand came out and swatted at him again. He saw it coming this time and ducked away. "Watch it, can't ya? I'm showing respect. I was hiding behind da elevator house, hanging off da edge."

The don suddenly stood up and looked angrily at the two men standing behind Walpole. "Did you look there?"

"They was all gone, boss." The soldier's voice became higher, his tense words running together. "We didn't know this guy would still be on the roof? We thought he left when the others took off."

His gloved fist closed around the handle of the war souvenir and he raised it in the air. "You *thought?* There's not enough brains between the two of you to think."

"Honest, boss, we didn't know!"

With a quick angry motion he slammed the knife tip into the desktop. Releasing it, the ornate blade vibrated making a humming sound in the quiet room. Walking around the desk, he ignored Walpole who was trying not to wet his pants and stood in front of the two men. "I do not tolerate mistakes," he said evenly. "You have seen what happens to those who incur my displeasure."

Walpole watched curiously, as the two large men began to tremble. "Give us another chance, boss," the larger one said. "It won't happen again, I swear!"

"Consider this your last warning." Suddenly, his rage abated and he turned back toward the desk and retrieved the dagger. Contemplating it, he said, "Francis was a sucker for the broads. That bitch somehow tricked him." Turning back he confronted them. "You find the woman and that little programmer and make sure there are no more copies of that disk." He glared angrily. "Management must remain anonymous at all cost." Pointing the dagger at the smaller man, he growled, "No loose ends. Do you understand me?"

"Yes sir," he said quickly, moving toward the door.

The larger man stood his ground. "Meaning no respect, sir," he said, "but we ain't got a clue on where to start. The house burnt down and they took off."

The don turned back toward Walpole. "You were with them in the car. Where are they residing?"

Walpole fixed his eyes on the dagger. "Day didn't trust me. Blindfolded me when day took me where day was staying." He could taste the fear in his mouth, as he spoke the lie. "Said day was droppin' me off and heading out of town."

With lightening speed, the knife flicked out and made a small slit in Walpole's shirt. "This is the truth?"

Walpole began to shake again. Nodding his head up and down vigorously, he stammered, "Near as I can figure, dat house day had me in is somewhere in da country, maybe fifteen or twenty miles from where your boys caught up wit us. Honest, day always blindfolded me."

"I've lost two more good men today," the don growled. He stabbed the blade back into the tabletop, sinking it in deeper, and glared at the two soldiers. "Is what he says true?"

"Well, he *was* blindfolded when we caught 'em that time. He got that right."

His eyes big as saucers, Walpole said, "I swear, I don't know where day was going. If I'm lying, I'm dying!"

"Very appropriately put." He forced the knife from the shredded tabletop and pointed it at the shorter guard. "When you find the woman and the programmer, kill them both and dispose of the bodies."

"Yes sir."

"And take this one with you."

"Wait, you're making a big mistake," Walpole whined pitifully.

Ignoring him, the don fixed his eyes back on the two uneasy soldiers. "And no mistakes this time."

As they started to put a gag in Walpole's mouth, he wrenched free. Words began to spill from his trembling lips. "Dam-it!" he yelled, "I can help you find dis Wielding person your guys is lookin' for. You *need* me!"

Suddenly, the soldiers froze. The don looked angrily at them. "You talk too much. I'll cut your tongues out for that."

"We never told him nothing about Wielding, boss. We never even mentioned his name."

Turning back, he grabbed Walpole's shirt and put the dagger against his throat. "How do you know that name? I warn you, no lies."

Thinking quickly, Walpole sputtered, "Dutton, Deputy Dutton; he asked me if I knew him. He said you'd pay money to find him."

"This constable has a big mouth. And what did you tell him?"

"I'd never heard of da guy before. Then I overheard da broad you had on da tower say he had some merchandise dat she wanted."

"And what would this merchandise she spoke of be?"

"She said diamonds. He's wanted by da feds for stealing 'em. He's a bad dude. He murdered some guy to get 'em."

The don contemplated this information for a second. "What's your part in this?"

"I just tought if day was up for grabs, I'd deal myself in, somehow."

"And just how did you plan to do that?"

"I tink I know what he looks like and how to find him. Got a better chance than most, anyways."

"How could you possibly do that?"

"Contacts." *He bought it!* "Important contacts, dat's how."

"You were no help delivering the disk. Now you expect me to believe you can produce Wielding?"

"You want him or not?"

Instantly, the don's gloved hand flew out and struck Walpole across the face. "Tie him up. The little fool is lying. Quickly, the small one tied a rope around Walpole's neck and began to wrap it around his body, while the large hood stuck a sock in his mouth. Before he could tie the gag in place, Walpole spit it out.

"I ain't lying! You're looking for a tall guy with dark hair and bushy eyebrows, right? Dat's what Wielding looks like, ain't it?"

The don put his hand up to stop them from continuing. "I'm listening."

CHAPTER EIGHTEEN

"What happened?" Hazel asked, as the old man in the baggy pants, came prancing through the office door. His body looked almost trim and fit as he stripped off the blue denim shirt he had been wearing. "Did you find it?"

"It's been a long time since I took anybody out. You should of seen me, Hazel. I popped those two so quick, they didn't even get a shot off."

She followed him down the hall and into the bedroom. "What are you going on about, you old fool. You haven't shot anybody since your commando days back in the forties."

He peeled the false eyebrows off and threw the floppy hat in the corner. "I tell you Hazel, they fell like clay pigeons! Forgot how good I really was."

"Damn-it, Harry! Tell me what the hell happened out there."

"Well, I did like we planned. I got to the field across from the tracks before I put on the floppy hat; and that sack full of cans was a good touch. A man on the sidewalk saw me getting out of the truck and turned away when he thought I was gonna put the bite on 'em for a hand out." He leaned over the sink in the small bathroom and washed the black out of his gray hair. "I looked enough like that Ted fellow to fool his mother."

"Who the hell did you shoot?"

"I'm gettin' to it," he said, stripping a shoulder holster off his skinny chest and dropping it on the bed.

"Who, damn-it? Who did you shoot?"

"Wait a second, will you?" He dried his hair with a dingy towel and grinned at her. "It was just like old times and I was back when I was behind them enemy lines. They couldn't get me then and they can't get me now. It was so great."

"Harry, if you don't tell me this instant," she said, pulling the handgun from its holster. "I'm gonna put a hole in you."

He gently removed the colt 45 from her hand. "Easy, that thing has a hair trigger."

"Well?"

"I'd been out there for about an hour when two guys came running across the tracks at me. When I ducked behind a boxcar they put a round in it just above my head." He slipped the pistol back into its sheath and placed it gingerly on the bed. "The door was open on the other side and I waited for 'em inside, see. Like shooting ducks in a barrel, it was. They never even *saw* me, Hazel."

Hazel grinned. "I told you the mob might be watching, that's what the disguise was for. Did you find that Bull Durham sack?"

"Naw but I did find a good can of beer, see?" He pulled it out of his pocket and smiled a toothless grin. "Blue Ribbon."

"You old fool. What are we going to do now? That kid knows more then he's letting on; might even suspect I can read Dragonfly's e-mail. And now that mob is after us."

Removing his baggy pants, he slipped back into his faded bib overalls. "The only ones that got a good look at me is dead. We're in the clear."

"There could have been other's watching, Harry."

"Let 'em come, I'll be ready." He hung the 45 in the closet out of sight around the corner on a nail. "I'll keep it right here where it's handy. Anyway, they'll be looking for that guy Ted, not me."

"Mark, that kid that came with him ain't no dummy. He might beat us to the bag."

"If it's still out there, you mean?"

"I think it is, Harry, or they wouldn't be hanging around. Who do you suppose they are anyway?"

"What difference does it make. I can handle 'em."

"That list he gave Dragonfly is where the answer is. There were a lot more names."

"Well Dragonfly will just have to decode some more of 'em, won't he." He sat on the bed and removed the tennis shoes. Wiggling his toes, he looked up at her with a knowing expression. "When that happens, we'll know."

She nodded. "That Ted fellow might know something too."

"Maybe I ought to ask him."

"You just stick to the grunt work old man, leave the planning part to me."

"I don't care if you was a Captain in intelligence, Hazel. There are things that I'm smart at too."

"I know that, Harry."

"Until I met you, I didn't take orders from no female. Now you got me jumping through hoops, and I don't even think twice about it."

"Harry, we go back a long way. Have I ever led you wrong?"

"Naw."

"You just do the easy stuff; I'll do the thinking."

In the motel room, the Mafia don strode back and forth in front of Walpole, an irritated expression on his face. "So, you do know Wielding's description."

Walpole looked back slyly. "What you want him for, anyways?"

"It is enough to say that he has information that I must have. Now you've bought a little more time with this piece of trivia." He nodded to the soldier who immediately left the room. "What are you proposing?"

He bought it! "I got a brother dat knows a cop wit connections. Helps me wit finding people dat's hard to find; you know, like bail bond skip-outs and guys dat ain't paying no alimony, dat kind of ting."

The don turned away in disgust. "This is obviously beyond your limited capabilities."

Walpole put his hand out and grabbed the don's sleeve. "No, really, I know he can help. He *owes* me."

With his gloved hand, the don gently removed Walpole's fingers from his sleeve. Evenly, he said, "Do you believe in predestination?"

"You mean, like if you was born to be shot, you'll never be hung?"

"Close enough. If you do not follow my instructions explicitly, I will be the one that personally causes this event to happen to you. Do you understand my meaning?"

"Don't worry. I ain't gonna do nothin' rash. Ain't ready to die yet, dat's for sure!"

The don looked down at the knife. Toying with it, he etched a new facet to the diamond scratched in the desktop. "You can live in moneyed grandeur if you find this Matthew J. Wielding."

"What kind of moneyed grandeur we talkin' 'bout here?"

"If you find him, you will be paid one hundred thousand dollars for your efforts."

"Dat much?" Talking faster, Walpole said, "My brother and me can find anybody, especially dem dat don't want to be found, know what I mean? Does Wielding have a social security number?"

"Not an active one. I would have found him myself."

"Den my brother and me will just have to scratch a little deeper, dat's all. Is he in da states?"

"He may have been seen today in your grubby little town of Monroe."

"Hey, then no prob-lem-o, we'll have him in a week, tops."

"You have two days, no longer."

"Wait a minute. If dat was him in Monroe, why ain't *you* caught him by now?"

"Apparently, my associates have certain limitations. Since the demise of Big Francis, it is obvious that we must keep a low profile. The local constabulary may have discovered his body by now."

"And I ain't wanted, so I can go anywheres wit-out being stopped." Walpole's eyes became shrewd. "See, you *do* need me."

"Be aware, that if you are picked up by the constabulary, we will know if you mention this conversation. We have informants everywhere."

"Hey, I ain't no fool. If I snitch, day'll tink I'm wit you guys; put me in da same cell. I ain't in to dat."

"Possibly you are not as dull-witted as I thought." He turned, pointing the knife at one of the soldier that was standing at the door. "Take him back to town and release him."

CHAPTER NINETEEN

The doorbell rang and Betty Ann froze. Who could that be? She peeped through the curtain and saw Deputy Dutton standing at the door in the bright sunshine. Ted fled the living room and took his stand in the hall around the corner. He listened intently as she opened the front door. "Why, my goodness, if it isn't Deputy Dutton! How are you today?"

He removed his gray smoky-the-bear hat with its gold colored lanyard. "Tolerable, ma'am, just tolerable."

"I'm sorry to hear that. Hope it's not anything too serious."

"Yes'um." He stood there without speaking as though he had forgotten why he came.

"Is there something I can help you with? I'm always happy to help the law when I can."

Looking apologetic, his walleye stared past her into the house. "It's about that old house across the street, ma'am. The one that blew up?"

"Yes?"

"It weren't no accident after all."

Betty Ann put her hand to her chest in mock astonishment. "What ever do you mean?"

"I told 'em them gas lines is always accidentin', but it was a bomb that done it this time."

"My goodness; you don't say?"

"Yes'um, sure was. Somebody set it off, all right. That's why I had to come back and tell you."

"Well thank you for bringing me such exhilarating information. I surely appreciate it." She started to close the door, and he put his hat out trying to get words to come before she could close it. She saw the movement and stopped. "Is there something else? You looked like you wanted to say something."

"Yes'um, they is."

"You are going to tell me that the men in that big black car I saw set it off, aren't you?"

"Naw, we don't know who done it yet. That's why I came back here." He rocked back on his heels and rested the hat on his huge belly. "Maybe you remembered something else that you didn't remember to tell me before?" Suddenly seeing a spot of chalk on his hat, he wiped the rim clean with the flat of his hand and then looked up sheepishly. "People is always remembering stuff that they forgot to remember the first time they didn't remembered that kind of stuff."

"Well, I don't think so."

"Anything ma'am. The sheriff is hounding me something awful to find something out that somebody remembered that he can go on. Anything at all would help."

"Well, I don't know if this will help much, but when I came out on the porch the house was blazing and that big black car was driving up the street. Does that help?"

"Yes'um, I mean, no ma'am."

"Did you ever find that person you were asking about? What was his name? Weldin, or Wielding or something like that?"

"Naw, he ain't showed up. I spec he's left this part of the country."

"Guess you won't get that big reward from the man in the long black car then."

He looked sadly at his shoes, then back up at her. "I seen him again and he asked me the very same thing. Told him that feller ain't around here, as far as I can tell." Then his face lit up. "Now he's looking for some kind of little computer kind of feller. You know them that works on the writing of it. He'll pay me a hundred dollars if I can find him."

"What's he want him for?"

"Didn't say, but he's gonna pay me a hundred dollars just to point him out." Rubbing the chalk spot on his hat again, he said, "Lady up the street said she saw a feller that sounded like him standing on your front porch the other day."

"What's this person look like?"

"He's a kind of youngish little feller, with black hair and he was wearing faded jeans and a T-shirt. The man in the long black car said his name was Mark."

"Oh, she must mean that person that rang my doorbell trying to sell me a subscription to some kind of gardening magazine. I didn't need it and I sent him away."

"Yes'um."

Betty Ann took a step toward the officer, an eager expression suddenly on her face. "Do you think that man would be willing to pay me if I helped him find this Mark person? Where does he live?"

The constable backed up a step. "Don't know ma'am. He somehow always finds me."

"Deputy Dutton, I could sure use the money"

"Just drives up in that big old black car. Never did find out where he stays." Backing farther away, he said, "Most likely somewhere in some big city like Monroe."

"Well, do you think he would?"

"Next time I see him, I'll be sure to ask him."

"Would you do that for me? I really do need the money."

Deputy Dutton hastily backed off the porch, almost falling on the steps. At the curb, he turned back, his hat still in his hand. "Doubt if I'll ever see him again, though."

Betty Ann waved from the porch. "I'd appreciate it a whole lot."

Chuckling, she closed the front door and grinned at Ted who had come back into the living room. "He's such an gullible old teddy bear."

"Don't underestimate him."

"What do you mean, Ted? He's just a sweet old dumb southern cop."

"Might be an act." Ted went to the window and peered out making sure that the constable had really left. "Deals with a lot of people."

Walking back to the kitchen, she poured Ted a cup of coffee and sat it on the table. "If he's that good, he should be on the stage in New York City."

Following her, he sat down at the table and stared into the cup. "Knows more than he's letting on."

"You mean coming here looking for Mark?"

"Uh-huh."

Betty Ann suddenly put her finger to her lips. "Shush, someone's on the front porch again!" She ran to the curtained window in the living room and peeped through. "It's Mr. Walpole!" Checking to make sure he had come alone, she opened the door before he could ring the bell. "Well, you sure came back in a hurry. Did you find the diamonds?"

"No, somebody beat me to 'em." He walked in quickly and closed the door, then looked through the window. "Hope I lost 'em."

Her eyebrows shot up. "Lost who? Certainly, you don't mean that gangster?"

"Yeah," he said, his apprehensive eyes searching the street. "Tink I out foxed 'em though." Walking into the kitchen, he sat down at the breakfast table.

"If you've led those terrible people to our doorstep!" She wagged her finger in his face, "I told you, you wouldn't find that little old bag."

"Well, I tink somebody did. Least ways I tink dat's what day had on 'em when day took off."

"You actually saw someone with the bag of diamonds?"

"Well he had somethin'. Anyways, two of da mob followed him around behind a freight car and got shot for their trouble. Say Ted, where'd you go after I left?"

Before he could speak, Betty Ann said, "We've all been right here. Why do you ask?"

Walpole suddenly looked relieved. "Well you ain't gonna believe dis." Then he told them about what happened on the bridge and his conversation with the don.

"You actually talked to that terrible person?"

His eyes danced with excitement. "Hey, does a hummy bird poop on the posies?"

"And he let you leave?" She shot a worried look at Ted. "I find that hard to believe! He ordered all of us killed at the tower."

"Yeah, well I made a deal wit him."

"A deal! Are you out of your mind? That same person we saw on the tower?"

"Dat's him. He's always wearin' gloves. Guess he don't want his fingerprints around nowheres."

"What kind of deal?" Ted asked, uneasiness in his voice.

"Well, if I find dis guy he's lookin' for, he'll pay big bucks." He looked at Betty Ann with a wry grin. "How you like dem apples?"

"Are you referring to Wielding?"

"Yeah lady, and Wielding's da one dat took out da two goons at da tracks, so he's close by somewheres."

"And you're sure it was Wielding?"

"The mob got a good look at him, Betty Ann. Day had 'em pegged down to his hair and eyebrows. Looked kind of like you Ted."

Betty Ann glanced at Ted and smirked, "And *he* found the diamonds! Can you imagine that Ted?"

Ted looked away. "Uh-huh."

"Well, I got only two days to finger him. Ain't got a clue of where to start." Walpole glanced at the dirty breakfast plates. "Any more eggs?"

"Damn!" Ted said, suddenly jumping to his feet. "They bugged you before!"

"Hey, not to worry. Already tought of dat." Walpole grinned. "First ting I done was to duck into a service station john and take off everyting. Almost didn't find it. It was stuck under my shirt collar." Licking his lips, he watched Betty Ann put bacon and eggs on a plate and set it down in front of him. "First, I tought about flushing it. But den it come to me, sudden like a horse fallin' out of da sky onto a outhouse." He took a mouth full of eggs and chewed while they waited. "There was dis cat outside, see, and I clipped da bug in its fur." He took another mouth full and chewed for a second, then stuffed the wad into the side of his jaw. "Den I chased it for almost a block, 'till dis stray dog got into da act. Should of seen 'em stampeding down da street. Probably still runnin'." He swallowed hard. "Den I took off da other way."

"How do you propose to find this Wielding person?"

"Don't have a clue, lady. Da don said he'd pay me a hundred large just to steer him in da right direction."

"A hundred thousand dollars?"

He studied Betty Ann's skeptical expression for a second. "You don't tink he'd do dat?"

"Do you?" Betty Ann said exasperation in her voice.

"Not in a million years. I just went along, lookin' for a chance to haul my tiny butt out into da street."

"You knew it' was another ruse?"

"Does champagne come wit a cork stopper?" He grinned self-confidently at Betty Ann. "Yeah, I knew. And if he bought my story, he's dumber than dirt. He was just playing along so he could follow me here."

"Sure there's no more bugs?" Ted asked.

"Hey, I'm sure. Ain't gonna risk dem finding dis place."

Ted went to the front window and looked out. "You better be right."

"Hitched a ride with some old dude. He was waiting at a stoplight in town. Gave me a ride all the way to Wingate."

"And you weren't followed?"

"I watched the road behind me all the way, like a hawk guarding chickens." He took another mouthful of eggs. "Most of the cars was heading west toward Monroe."

Betty Ann looked nervously at Ted. "How do you know the nice old gentleman wasn't one of his gang?"

"He wasn't from around here, England maybe." He took the last bite of bacon, and chewed thoughtfully on it. "Talked like one of dem guys in da movies. Watched him head on down 74 toward Marshville. Said something about it being sweet sorrow or something like that, but he had to leave."

"Parting is such sweet sorrow?"

"Yeah, dat was it. Weird huh?"

"Ted, he was quoting Shakespeare!"

Ted looked grim.

CHAPTER TWENTY

On the fifth floor of the old hotel in downtown Monroe, a man sat patiently at a window in a darkened room, a ring of cigarette butts scattered around his ladder-back chair. Binoculars at the ready, he suddenly flinched as the telephone beside him jangled. Quickly picking it up, he mumbled into it, "Yes ... just returned." He placed his half-smoked cigarette in an ashtray resting on the well-worn chest of drawers beside a sagging bed. "Heating up," he said. "Two people grabbed an individual near the monument ... don't know, never saw him before ... no, *not* the General. Too short."

The binoculars shot to his eyes and he studied a figure that had just stepped out of a doorway. Then he relaxed and the glasses fell back catching on the strap around his neck. "They were gone before we could follow ... yes, we think Wielding was here today ... it's just a matter of time." Relaxing, he leaned back in the chair. "Dental records? ... Well, I maintained *that* all along, old boy; the body in the river was *not* General Fitzhammer's. If your people had listened to me in the first place ... Your informant seems correct; the general took their money, then reneged on delivery." He picked up the cigarette, Russian style, with his thumb and forefinger, brought it to his thin lips, pulled smoke into his lungs, then quickly released it into the stale air. "God Rest Our Confederate Soldiers will bring him here ... I wager it will be sooner ... and Wielding will lead us to Fitzhammer."

Leaning forward in his chair he studied the people below again while listening to the voice on the phone. "The don obviously wants his share ... twenty million in diamonds is a lot of incentive to kill. When Fitzhammer and the don meet we'll be ready ... Wielding took out two on the tracks today ... maybe the actor will have to put in another appearance."

Harry pranced down the smoky hallway at the insurance office. "Wait 'till you hear this, Hazel!"

"What is it now, Harry? Can't you see I'm busy?" She took a pull from the cigarette hanging in the corner of her mouth and blew smoke in his face. "I'm trying to pay bills here."

Waving the smoke away, he crowed, "Maybe you should listen to me once in a while, Hazel. I just found out something that could make us rich."

"Sure, you have. Another one of those pyramid schemes?" She turned her back and picked up a utility bill from the counter and frowned at it.

"Listen to me, will ya, Hazel? Just got off the phone with Moon."

She turned back and smirked at him. "Oh, and my brother's gonna make us rich? Don't make me laugh; he's dumber than dirt." Cigarette dangling in the corner of her mouth, she chuckled, "Dumber than dirt." Spitting in a tin can that still had the Pinto Bean label on it, she said, "Why a smart woman like Avis ever married him, I'll never figure out."

"Go ahead, laugh it up old woman, but he might be onto something this time."

"What's he said that's got you so worked up, Harry?"

He grinned slyly. "He's been in contact with a feller that is willing to pay big bucks for information on a John he's looking for."

"So, what's that got to do with us?"

"The individual he's looking for fits the same description as one of the two that showed up over here the day of the fire."

"You mean that Mark kid?"

"No, the other one. The one with the half-moon scar on his chin."

Taking a last pull on her cigarette, she dropped it on the floor and stepped on it. "What kind of money, Harry?"

"A guy in a limo told him that he'd pay $100,000."

"Bull. And you bought that?"

"Moon talked to him several times and the man always shows up in a stretch limo with a fancy chauffeur. That sounds like big money to me."

Hazel folded her arms across her stomach and squinted through the smoke at him. "What'd you tell him?"

"Not a word, Hazel." He grinned shrewdly. "Why let Moon and Avis in on it. We know how to contact that Mark kid, and he knows how to get hold of the other one. What do you think now?"

She stared out through the dirty front window. "Sounds too good to be true. Why would he pay that kind of money?"

"Moon thought it had to do with a hidden stash or something like that."

"How we gonna find the man in the limo?"

"That could be the tricky part, Hazel. He just shows up on his own, Moon says."

"You know, Moon could be holding back, not telling you everything."

"Yeah, I thought of that. But he swears he don't know how to find the limo guy, don't even know his name."

"Maybe I'll call Avis. Moon don't keep anything from her, she won't put up with it."

Harry chuckled. "Yeah, when he told me they was getting married, I warned him she was way too smart for him, and she'd never let him get away with nothing."

Hazel lit another cigarette. Holding the match stick, she stared shrewdly into the little flame. "We might need to deal Moon and Avis in on this one, Harry." Blowing out the match, she grinned. "You tell Moon that the next time he sees that man in the limo, tell him we have information for him about the one he's looking for. To come by the office if he's interested."

"Well, what do you think now, was I right or what?"

Absentmindedly, she picked a fragment of tobacco from the tip of her tongue. "In the meantime I'll get Dragonfly to lure the kid out. He sounds like a rich sucker with more money than brains."

"I told you, Hazel, we're gonna get rich. Don't forget I told you."

CHAPTER TWENTY-ONE

Mark came into the kitchen looking puzzled as Betty Ann was putting the last of the supper dishes into the dishwasher. "Dragonfly sent another e-mail." She looked up. "Wants me to meet him at that diner across from the insurance office tonight."

Ted looked up from his newspaper. "Why tonight?"

"He says it's urgent. He's decoded more names."

Betty Ann dried her hands on her apron. "Why doesn't he just send it like he did before?"

"I asked him that. Said it's too dangerous. He says we need to talk in person."

"Last time he didn't show, remember?"

"I think he'll be there this time, Betty Ann."

She glanced warily at Ted. "What do you think, Ted?"

He shrugged. "You willing to risk it, Mark?"

"Will you drive me, Ted?"

"Oh, can I come along too? I'm dying of curiosity. Please, Ted. I'm getting cabin fever cooped up in here."

"What about the mob?"

"We'll take the rental. They won't see us behind the tinted windows. Please, Ted."

"You'll stay in the car?"

"In the car?" She scowled at him. "That's no fun."

"Till I know it's safe."

"Oh, all right, I promise." She started down the hall, talking to herself as she went. "I'll wear the dark dress."

"Might not hurt to take along the Uzi," Mark said, when she was out of hearing range.

"Already in the trunk."

"What about Walpole?"

"Leave him sleeping."

South Boulevard was crowded with going home traffic as Ted pulled the rent-a-car into a vacant unlit parking lot. A half block away the glass facade of Mom's Diner, across from Hazel's insurance office, reflected back an eerie green and orange glow from a string of raw colored bulbs on top of the doublewide. Like grotesque Christmas adornments, they boldly proclaimed INSURANCE - CHEAP.

"That's the diner, Ted?"

"Yeah."

"And we're parking way out here?"

"What's the problem?"

"Why didn't you use that lot behind the restaurant?"

"Darker here."

"But that one's closer; I want to see."

"What if it's a trap?"

"Oh!"

Ted and Mark got out. Before Ted shut the door, he warned, "Keep it locked."

"Don't worry," she said. "Look at this sleazy neighborhood! You think I'm crazy?" He shut the car door, and she watched the two men work their way around behind the restaurant and enter through the back door.

Taking a seat by the window, Mark picked up a menu and casually read it. Ted muttered, "Where's your Dragonfly?"

"Told him I'd sit near the front and be wearing this blue shirt."

Fifteen minutes went by while Ted played with a book of matches with Mom's Diner printed on the flap. Waitresses scurried between the kitchen and their assigned tables ignoring the two men. "Aught-ah be here by now."

"Don't worry, Ted. This is kind of exciting. We're finally gonna meet Dragonfly face to face."

"Yeah, Exciting" Ted said sarcastically, trying to watch both doors at the same time. Suddenly, he saw a familiar face. Dropping the matchbook into his shirt pocket, he nudged Mark under the table with his foot. A wiry old man wearing ragged cut-off bib overalls and beach flip-flops came in the front and looked in their direction. Then he shuffled over to the table.

"You're Mark, ain't cha?" he said, a frozen snaggletooth grin on his face.

Astonished, Mark said, "You're Dragonfly?"

"Naw, and I ain't no butterfly neither." The grin never left, but suddenly he didn't seem quite as frail as Ted had remembered. "He sent me to tell ya to wait rat cheer. He'll be along directly." Pulling up a chair from a nearby table, Harry turned it around and sat down in it the wrong way, his legs straddling it and his arms on the backrest. Resting his chin on the back of his hand, he stared at them, still grinning.

"I've never met Dragonfly in person," Mark said. "What's he look like?"

"Me neither. Talked to 'em on the phone once," he said, "What y'all want him fer?"

Ted stared back. "It's personal."

"Well, he'll be along any minute now; told me so, his self."

"We can't wait long," Ted said, looking at his watch. "You have his phone number?"

"Never gave me none."

"What's your name?" Ted asked, his voice developing an edge.

"Harry, what's your-en?"

Ted ignored the question and looked toward a waitress. He raised his hand. She came over with her note pad poised to take an order.

Harry, still grinning, tried to wave her away. "Y'all ain't got no time."

"I'll take the time," Ted growled. "Coffee." Ignoring Harry he looked toward Mark, "How about you?" Mark shook his head and looked uneasy.

The waitress poured coffee into a mug and placed in front of Ted. Remembering him and the good tip from their last visit, she smiled. "Anything else?" Ted shook his head. Disappointed, she dropped a ticket on the table and walked away.

From his view at the window, Mark could see their car in the dark parking lot with Betty Ann sitting in the front seat. "Where's Dragonfly? It's getting late."

"Won't be long now, sonny," Harry said, following Marks eyes out the window.

Mark frowned; Harry's silly grin was beginning to irritate him.

Across the street, the stretch limo pulled into the dark gas station lot beside Hazel's Insurance Office and parked. Two thugs stepped out and made sure that the way was clear before opening the passenger door for the tall man in the expensive suit. "I'll go in and speak to this Hazel person alone. Wait out front ... out of sight ... and keep your eyes open." Stepping up on the small front porch, he entered the office, and stopped at the front counter.

Hazel had been watching Harry talking to Mark and Ted from her bedroom window. Hearing the door open, she quickly put down her powerful binoculars and limped down the hallway to the front. As she came into view, the blond ends of her stringy gray hair resting on her overstuffed blue denim shift created the illusion of someone not very bright.

"You are Hazel?" the don asked.

"Uh-huh. You the one that's been talking to my brother, Deputy Dutton?"

"Your brother? Yes."

Her watery eyes stared vacantly at him. "He says you'll pay money if I can put the finger on some guy for you."

"That is correct. If your information is accurate." His cold blue eyes gazed back, disdainfully.

"How much?"

"That would depend on how precise your information might be."

"Moon ain't always right on what he says. Who we talking about, here?"

Hesitating, he brushed an imaginary speck of lint from his dark pinstriped suit. Contemptuously he said, "First you tell me. If your information is important enough for me to proceed with this conversation, then perhaps I will continue."

Her shrewd eyes stared back at him cautiously. "You're looking for a kid named Mark, right?"

He nodded his head perceptibly. "Continue."

"How much you willing to pay?"

The edge in his voice disappeared. "The constable was promised one hundred dollars for information leading to his location. I would offer you the same enticement."

Hazel grinned slyly. "How much if I showed him to you personally? Like so close that you can reach out and touch him?"

"If you actually deliver him into my hands, two hundred dollars would not be beyond my anticipated expenditures."

"Uh-huh, well I have, uh, anticipated expenditures of my own. What about, say three big ones?"

"Three thousand dollars!" His gloved hand clenched into a fist. "Is this some kind of hillbilly scam? I warn you woman, I will not be trifled with."

Suddenly, her demeanor changed. She no longer was the simpleton he thought he had been addressing. Through clenched teeth she growled, "Back off, Big Shot. You don't scare me. You interested, or not?"

"You stupid cow! Obviously, you are not aware of who you are addressing. I can have you killed, leave no trace for the authorities to find."

Hazel stood her ground. "Look Big Shot, I deal with all kinds. Been threatened by bruisers that would make you wet your pants. I'm still here, get my meaning?"

"Is that so." The don turned toward the door, preparing to call in his men.

Before he could, Hazel said, "You told Moon you'd pay a hundred thousand. That's a lot more than I'm asking for, Big Shot."

He swung back around, making no effort to control the irritation in his voice. "The one hundred thousand was not offered for this Mark person."

"Oh yeah? Who then?"

"That is entirely another matter and no concern of yours. It is inconceivable that you could help me there."

"You're sure about that, Big Shot?"

"Obviously, you are wasting my time." He turned away again.

Hazel's irritating laugh filled the small room. "Go ahead Big Shot. But I know a damned sight more than you think I do."

Intrigued by her insolence, he paused. "You do have a certain boldness I admire." Turning back toward her, he sneered, "or maybe it's just your doltish nerve."

Hazel laughed again, not offended. "I thought we could do business. Who's the John you're hunting?"

"I will tell you this much. I am looking for a man, about my age, who does not fit the description of the person we have been negotiating for. He is tall, and his name is Matthew J. Wielding, but he may be using an alias."

"Uh-huh." Hazel paused and lit a cigarette. The smoke streamed from her nostrils as her hard eyes fixed on the man standing in front of her. "Does he have a half-moon shaped scar on his chin?"

The don's eyes widened and he stepped back a step. "You know of this person?"

Triumphantly, she said, "How much for the both of 'em?"

"You can produce both these individuals? Is this possible?"

"I said I could. How much, Big Shot?"

"One-hundred thousand dollars if you can do what you say."

"It'll take more than that." She grinned evilly at him. "If I can put 'em both in your hands right here, tonight, will you up the ante, Big Shot?"

Angrily, he pounded his gloved fist on the counter top. "Stop calling me that!" Hazel smirked back at him, knowing that her insults were keeping him off balance. His eyes became wild. "I warn you, if you are lying …"

"How much, Big Shot? I want to hear you say it."

"You try my patience, woman."

"I can get 'em both for you tonight, but I gotta see your money first. You dealing or not?"

"All right, I'll bump the pot by fifty thousand if you deliver them both tonight. But no tricks, I warn you."

Hazel grimaced. "Oh you want 'em bad, don't you. I can see it in your eyes."

He glared at her, his gloved hand clenching and unclenching. "Where are they?"

"Here's the deal, when you first lay eyes on 'em, fifty big ones goes into my pocket, then a hundred more when I hand 'em over. Is it a deal?"

The don nodded. "You drive a hard bargain."

"Then lets see your money, Big Shot."

"Your merchandise first," he hissed.

Taking her time, as she watched his exasperation increase, she dropped her lit cigarette on the floor and slowly put it out with her shoe. "Okay, wait here." Calmly, she walked down the hall, leaving him standing in front of the counter. Shortly she returned holding something behind her back. Tensing, the don withdrew an automatic pistol from an inside pocket. "Put away the piece. This ain't no weapon. Show me the green."

Leveling the firearm at her, he snarled, "Would I be so foolish as to carry it on me?"

"Like the kids say, I'll show you mine, if you'll show me yours."

His hand began to tremble. "I can see you will not be dissuaded. Would you consider some other form of gratuity, rather than hard cash?"

Hazel regarded him warily. "I doubt it, but I'm listening."

"For emergencies only, you understand, I carry on my person, something far more valuable than the vulgar green paper that you aspire to."

"Ain't nothing better than greenbacks, Big Shot. Nothing."

He pulled a soft leather bag from his inside pocket. "Perhaps you might consider these," he said, dumping a pile of sparkling diamonds onto the counter top. "Easier to transport and a universal currency."

Hazel's eyes popped open. "So, you found 'em after all!"

With the tip of his pistol, he spread the little jewels out on the counter top. "Several years ago, this bag was appraised at seven-hundred thousand American. I will divide it into four bright little piles. You may pick the accumulation of your choice."

"If these are real ..." Hazel's voice trailed off, as she stared, fascinated at the sight in front of her. "Sorry I gave you a hard time."

"Use my glass, inspect their clarity, their color; see for your self how they sparkle. They are genuine and of the very finest quality, I can assure you."

Hazel took the glass and inspected one of the larger stones. "Yeah, I can live with this! Gimme that first bunch." She reached for it, but the don quickly pushed her hand away with the tip of the pistol.

"I've shown you mine," he said evenly. "Now, you show me yours." He quickly raked the other three piles back into the leather bag, leaving the rest on the table. "You may keep that large stone in your possession as security until our contract has been completed."

"Then come out on the porch," Hazel said, handing him the powerful binoculars. She pointed at the diner across the street. "Look at that second window."

"Focusing the binocular on the three at the table, without taking his eyes away, he said under his breath, "I am amazed at your resourcefulness." Quickly, he motioned to the two men standing in the shadows that Hazel had failed to notice. "Tony, take this pig back into her sty. But first, I'll take that," he said, snatching the diamond from her hand.

"Hey! What about our deal?"

"Certainly, you must be jesting. Why should I pay you now? When I dispose of the two in the restaurant, there will be room in the pit for you as well." Turning to the larger soldier, he snarled, "Watch her closely." Then, quickly, he and his accomplice walked across the street toward the diner.

CHAPTER TWENTY-TWO

In the diner, Harry suddenly stood and quickly walked toward the back exit. Mark looked up. "Where's he going?" Then he saw the don coming toward their table, a pistol held at his side. Before Mark had time to react, he was standing behind Ted's chair.

Leaning over, he said in a low voice, "The hard object you feel pressed between your shoulder blades is a pistol. I will not hesitate to fire at the slightest provocation."

Ted looked at Mark. "It's that guy from the tower, Ted."

Across the street, Tony dragged Hazel into the office and shoved her behind the counter. "Stay put and I won't tie you up." She leaned against the counter, glaring at him. She didn't appear to be frightened or even excited. "What's with you, lady?" Suddenly, Tony noticed the little pile of glittering diamonds on the counter top. Mesmerized, he stared at them.

Hazel smiled. "They're real all right, and worth thousands, maybe millions," she said, her voice dripping honey. "Why don't we split 'em? You know, take 'em and make a run for it." He licked his lips, thinking it over, as Hazel's hand found Harry's pistol secreted on the shelf behind the counter. Earlier, just in case, she had hidden it there for just such an emergency. Her finger on the hair trigger, she hastily raised the weapon toward the gangster. Before she could take aim it went off. The bullet passed through the big man's shoe and lodged into the floor.

"You shot me," he screamed, grabbing his foot and dancing around on one leg. "Damn-it!"

"The next one goes in your bellybutton big boy. Get yourself in that closet over there. I can't miss from here." Ignoring her, he fell to the floor holding his shoe. Blood oozed through a neat little hole. Coolly, she opened the closet door and motioned with the pistol. "Stop your bellyaching. Get in there; you're gonna live. That's more than your boss had planned for me." Tony crawled inside. Ignoring his groans she closed and locked the door. Then, chuckling under her breath, she slipped to the front door and peeped outside. "But you ain't gonna dance the tango for a while."

In the restaurant, the patrons heard the muffled shot and the hum of conversation came to a stop. Tensely, the don whispered, "Both of you get up slowly and move toward the front door. I will follow behind you." The don's nervousness suddenly peaking and he hissed, "NOW!" As they maneuvered through the crowded diner and through the front door, he held the pistol out of sight, just inside his jacket.

Their waitress seeing them leaving followed the three men outside. "Sir, you haven't paid your check yet."

The frenzied gangster, ignoring her plea, hissed at Ted, "Keep walking." By now the pistol was pressed tight against Ted's back.

Unaware of the weapon, she reached out and grabbed the mobster by the sleeve. "I'm calling the police!" Holding on, she yelled, "Help, somebody, help!"

"Don't touch me," he shrieked. Turning, he fired point blank into her body. She fell against the porch railing, leaving a dark trail of blood as she slipped to the floor.

At a table near the door, a surprised off duty policeman, stood and brought his service revolver up. The don fired first. Immediately, diners screamed and bolted for the back door.

Giggling hysterically, the mafia chieftain discharged his pistol into the crowd. "Stop that screeching. Stop it!" It only grew louder. He fired again. More people fell. A little girl sat on the floor holding a doll in her arms, stared blankly back at him. Suddenly, his killing frenzy subsided and he turned away. The acrid odor of cordite replacing the pleasant aroma of southern cooking as he muttered, "I will not have it!"

At the first sound of gunfire, Ted pushed Mark in front of him and they sprinted toward the corner of the building. The don turned and fired, his bullet splintering a tree limb above Mark's head. As they rounded the corner the second gangster stood blocking their escape. A split second later, the don came charging up. Hyperventilating, he hissed through clenched teeth, "I should kill you now."

The soldier pointed his pistol at Mark, hesitated, then at Ted. "You want I should, boss?"

"No," he said, his emotions suddenly back under control. "The authorities can't be far behind. Escort them back to the limousine." He cocked his head at the sound of a siren in the distance. "They haven't wasted any time," he muttered. Reaching the relative safety behind the limo, the don pushed the pistol into Mark's stomach. He cocked it and growled, "The disk, I will have it now!"

"I don't have it anymore."

The sound of sirens increased. "Those records were for my eyes only!"

Mark could feel the cold steel against his stomach. "It was just a bunch of meaningless numbers to me."

"I will not be dissuaded. Give it to me NOW!"

"He's telling you the truth," Ted said, sirens wailing, now just a block away.

"Why should I believe you?"

Ted growled, "Because he gave it to Dragonfly."

The don turned the weapon toward Ted. "I'll kill you where you stand. Where is this illusive Dragonfly?"

Mark saw the frustration in his face; knew that he was going to fire. Quickly, he said, "We were here to meet him at the diner. I've never seen him in person, but Hazel has." The don's eyes narrowed as the sound of sirens filled their ears. "She set up the meeting," Mark said, "she knows how to find him."

The don grinned evilly. "This has suddenly become easier." Pushing them into the limo, he shut the door and turned to the soldier. "You and Tony bring the old hag back here to me. Go quickly!"

As the soldier left, the don tensely watched the scene across the street. Police cars arrived. People milled around. Someone crouched over the still form of the waitress. No one seemed to notice the limo in the shadowy obscurity of the service station lot.

Suddenly, the don's soldier came back with the wounded guard in tow. As they reached the limo, Tony's injured foot gave way and he fell, grabbing onto the hood ornament. Hanging on, he said, "She ain't there no more, boss."

"What?" he said. He grabbed Tony by the throat. "How could you let this happen?"

Panting in pain, he gritted his teeth and said, "Shot me in the foot. Locked me in a closet"

"And my diamonds; my beautiful diamonds?"

"They was real?"

"Yes, they were real, you idiot."

"Gone." Tony looked fearfully into the face of the enraged Mafia chief. "Never seen so many piled up before, boss. I didn't know."

"They were there only as an enticement, you fool. She was not supposed to *keep* them." Frustrated, he pounded his gloved fist onto the top of the limo. Then he pulled the pistol from his belt. "Imbecile! I'm surrounded by imbeciles!" Stepping closer, he shoved his weapon against Tony's belly and pulled the trigger, the muffled noise sounding no louder than the traffic noises on the boulevard. "I warned you!"

Surprise on his face, Tony reached out, clutching at the don's shoulder for support. "I didn't know, boss."

Coldly, the don stepped back and watched him fall to the ground. Turning to the other soldier, he said, "Get us out of here."

Seconds later, the limo slipped out into traffic. Unnoticed, it casually moved past the diner. "Slowly, slowly," the don said to the uneasy driver. "To those fools we're just another observer to their little drama." Two blocks down, the limo turned the corner.

Betty Ann, in the rent-a-car, nervously chewed on a fingernail and pulled out into traffic. Keeping the long black car's distinctive taillights in sight, she followed behind at a discrete distance.

CHAPTER TWENTY-THREE

On a side street, not far from the insurance office, Harry slipped through the back door of a rundown boarding house. He entered a small paint-flaked three-room apartment. Hazel didn't look up. She was perched on an old double bed with a magnifying glass in her hand. Squinting and pulling hard on a cigarette, she leaned over, and blew smoke at a collection of sparkling diamonds scattered across the dark surface of the smooth blanket. "Look at this, would you, Harry."

"You found the Bull Durham sack?"

"Hell no, Harry. This is what that crazy fool gave me for fingering that kid Mark and his big buddy."

"Good Lord, Hazel! We hit the mother load. Must be half a million worth."

Hazel looked shrewdly at Harry, her greedy eyes dancing. "This is just a fourth of what he had on him, Harry."

He picked up a large stone and held it to the light inspecting it. "And he gave you all these?"

She grinned at him impishly and took another drag on her cigarette. "Well, he didn't exactly *give* 'em to me, Harry. I kind of took 'em."

"Damn, why didn't you get 'em all?"

"Didn't have the chance. He kept the rest on him."

"Wish I'd of known. Might of stayed around and relieved him of the rest."

"Why'd you take off, anyway, Harry? That wasn't the plan."

"Well a good run is better than a bad stand, you know?" Looking away, he bounced the diamond in his hand, estimating its weight.

"What the hell does that mean, Harry?"

"When I seen him coming across the street, think he had a piece in his hand; couldn't tell for sure, but I decided not to stick around and find out."

"He had one all right. Planned on using it on me. Good thing I had yours stashed behind the counter."

"If I'd of had it, I wouldn't of left so soon."

"That's how I got these." She raked her hand through the pile, watching them glitter. Snickering, she said, "Shot this guy in the foot. Should of seen him doing the fox trot."

Harry grinned. "Everybody heard it over there. Wondered what was going on."

She pulled on her cigarette again. "After I put him in the closet, I took some of our stuff and headed over here, just in case."

Harry frowned. "There was a lot of shooting going on after I left the diner, could hear it near a block away." He put the diamond back on the bed. "I'd of been right in the middle of it if I'd stayed around."

"Yeah, I heard it. Most likely those two he was looking for. That blue eyed dude thought he was something special. Had several flunkies along just to back him up."

"Think he's connected, Hazel?"

"Naw. Mafiosi don't talk educated like he did. He does have some muscle though and I wasn't about to fight 'em all."

Harry looked worried. "We better take these little beauties and get the hell out of Dodge, know what I mean?"

"What's your hurry? No body knows about this place."

"I mean, if he really does have juice, Hazel."

"We can handle anything he can throw at us. I got one in the foot and you took out them two at the yard. How smart can they be anyhow?"

Harry pointed at the diamonds. "He ain't gonna be too happy about you runnin' off with these here."

"So what?" She took a last drag on the cigarette and dropped it into a half-filled drinking glass on the nightstand, and grinned up at him. "What good's happiness anyway? It ain't gonna buy him no money, is it?"

Harry chuckled but still looked uncomfortable. "Glad we kept this place for a fall back." He ran his hands over the glittering stones and leered at Hazel. "Too bad we missed them others."

Grinning back, she said, "We may get 'em yet, Harry. I've got a plan."

CHAPTER TWENTY-FOUR

Inside the limo, bulletproof glass separated Ted and Mark from the two men up front. Back doors, locked and controlled from the front, made it impossible to escape. "You ditched this limo at the airport, Ted."

"Different one."

"How many they got, anyway?" Ted shrugged and looked out the window, watching the scenery go by. Leaving the Charlotte area behind, the limo traveled down highway 74, past the Monroe Mall, eventually turning off onto an unpaved country road near the Wingate tower. Then it turned again onto an overgrown winding path that snaked through a dense stand of trees and came to a stop at a tall chain link fence with a locked heavy iron gate.

Two minutes later, they crossed a narrow bridge spanning a stream. Halfway up the rise their headlights lit up a three-story farmhouse nestling close against a hill and the limo parked in the tall grass.

His pistol at the ready, the don motioned them out into a night fragrant with honeysuckle and magnolia blossoms. "You will find the accommodations less than you would like, but in time, you will learn to adjust."

Mark stumbled out into the darkness to the sound of crickets chirping. Not far away, a bullfrog's low-pitched groan sounded to Mark like some ominous prehistoric beast. "Where are we?" he ask.

"Merely an old farm. A relic of an uncomplicated time when the simple necessities of life were water from a springhouse down by that stream and a privy on the path behind the house. Of course you will visit neither of these. For you, there are other accommodations." Shinning a powerful flashlight into Ted's eyes, he said, "So we meet again."

"Have we met before?"

"Briefly. But before evoking the past, there is another matter. Your young friend has some explaining to do." He turned the bright beam onto Mark. "You broke my password codes. How?"

"It was an accident. I was just fooling around on my computer."

"Just fooling around? Who else knows about your fooling around?"

"I told Dragonfly, he knows. That's how it all got out of hand. He said there was money in it for us."

"Dragonfly, Dragonfly, everything comes back to this elusive Dragonfly. And you have no idea who or where he is?"

"Hazel knows. Why don't you ask her?"

"I intend to do that at my first opportunity." He turned to the guard. "You stay here and keep watch. I will return soon." As he herded Mark and Ted ahead of him up the hill, he said, "No one has lived here for many years. You will have the honor of being the first to clear away the cobwebs." The limo head lights made walking easy until they reached the steps leading to the front porch. Ted started to climb. "Not that way. Around to the side."

Reaching a dark root cellar under the back porch, the don shoved Mark forward into Ted and together they stumbled inside. Ted whispered to Mark, "Be ready when I make my move." Mark suddenly recoiled and fell back against Ted as a large rat scurried across the uneven dirt floor. It disappeared into the darkness.

The don chuckled, "Merely a hungry rodent. Soon, that will be the least of your worries. Keep moving." He pointed his light toward the far wall. A large dowel protruded from between two moldy planks near the ceiling. "Ah, just as I remembered." Pointing his pistol at Ted, he ordered, "Pull that spike down."

Ted pushed through the spider webs and yanked on the spike. A portion of the wall came forward and behind the concealed door he could see a dark passageway. "What's this?"

"You will be the first to walk in these shafts since the slave driver's whelp made his final journey. He went in, but never came out." He pushed Mark ahead of him and together they entered the silent musty cavern. Following Ted along the footpath beside a narrow gauge track that had once carried a hand truck hauling ore from deep within the hill, Mark shivered and asked, "Who didn't come out?"

The don's voice became bitter. "The old wolf, of course. He spent his entire life in here ... forcing others to dig ... never relenting ... always burrowing deeper and deeper into this accursed hill."

Mark hung onto Ted's shirttail, shuddering at the moldy odor escaping from the crumbling walls. "Is this a gold mine?" he asked.

"At one time a very profitable one. A fat vein gleamed and glittered in the white rocks at the time of its discovery by the very first slave driver. With the first gold, he bought this land, and built the house outside. He erected that fence and gate to keep the world at bay, to protect his secret find."

The don prodded Mark with the pistol barrel. "Follow your comrade."

Soon, they left the protection of the shored up ceiling and entered a smaller passageway. As they descended down the narrow crumbling excavation deeper into the mountain, the ceiling gradually became lower. Ted was forced to lean forward to keep from bumping his head. "Don't touch the walls, Mark," he warned. "Stay on the path."

Feeling a claustrophobic panic rising, Mark strained to catch his breath in the stale air. The walls seemed to be closing in around him. He drew back in terror. The don jabbed him again with his pistol. Frantically, Mark grabbed onto Ted's shirttail again.

"That's a good little soldier," the don said, "follow the Sergeant." Like fireflies from hell reflecting in his light beam, sand began to fall. "When the mother lode petered out, the old wolf spent the rest of his life down here, digging these passages, continuously looking for the next vein ... always the next one ... I thought it would never end."

Suddenly there was a grinding sound that filled the cavern. Falling back against Mark, in the dim light from the torch, Ted watched loose earth cascading down from a hole in the ceiling.

"It's a cave in!" Mark yelled, turning back up the path.
The don stood, like a statue, blocking his way. "Stay where you are, soldier." The dust cleared and he shoved Mark with his pistol again. "Around the pile, follow the Sergeant." Ted disappeared into the dark and Mark followed. "Before the old wolf died, his only son, brought up working in these crawl spaces, carried on the slave driver's work."

Suddenly, Mark bumped into Ted who was stopped at the edge of a drop-off. He whispered, "Keep him talking."

Shying away from the dark pit, Mark asked, "How did he die?"

"Murdered by his own whelp. Pushed him down that shaft behind you."

"He killed his own father?"

"He deserved to die."

"His own father?"

The don grinned evilly back at him. "It was to become a family tradition." Mark tried to move away from the dark hole, but the don shoved him closer. "As the son became an old man himself, with the same self-deception as his daddy, he realized he must have help. So on a dark cruel night, he stole into a nearby community and kidnapped a twelve-year old boy. Brought him back here to slave in the mine, just as he had done when he was young. Then the old man's son became the new slave driver, the *new* old wolf."

Mark whispered to Ted, "He keeps calling you Sergeant!"

"The slave driver's son still haunts these crawl spaces. You will meet him soon."

Suddenly, Mark understood. "And that kidnapped twelve year old boy was you?"

Unexpectedly the don retreated back up the tunnel several steps. "Yes, and I killed the old bastard right where you're standing." He pointed his light at the deep dark chasm behind Ted. Glowed faintly in the dark, a narrow decayed plank lay across it. The don's voice suddenly became colder. "You won't escape me this time, Sergeant."

Ted heard the unmistakable click of the pistol's hammer cocking and all at once he knew. "It's you!" He steeled himself for the bullet.

"When I threw those diamonds to you, I expected you would be captured with them in your possession. That would have been the final proof that was needed. But somehow you escaped my trap."

"Your face is different."

"A good job, don't you think? I wouldn't let them change my eyes though. Until now, no one has ever suspected. Gloves camouflaged my missing fingers. Tried to have them replaced, but it was not to be. Now batting in the glove takes their place."

"Face had me fooled."

"With you gone, there will be no one left to identify me. No one to proclaim the General is still alive." He aimed the weapon at Ted's head. "The long search for you is ended. I think I will miss it."

"What about the military?"

"They think I'm dead. They would have found you long ago, if I hadn't thrown them off your trail with false leads. I couldn't take the risk that someone might believe your story." Pointing the light back at the board across the abyss, General Fitzhammer said, "Now you will walk the plank, just as I did and the son of the old slave driver did before me. He took his chances on the board and failed, I was luckier."

Ted stepped gingerly across the teetering plank and Mark, holding to his shirttail, followed close behind him. On the other side, Mark's legs gave way under him and he fell onto the sandy soil. "He's crazy, Ted!"

"Some might say that," the General said, "but I'll be alive long after you're both dead and forgotten." Without warning, he pulled the board over to his side. "The only way out is back across this shaft. I discovered that fact many years ago as a young boy. That tiny space was my prison for many nights."

"One question, General."

"I suppose I owe you that much, Sergeant."

"Are you really a don, or is that another deception?"

"Oh yes. I bought my way into the Mafia with part of the diamonds. Once I was in, the leaders conveniently died off one at a time."

"And Corsair Enterprises is yours?"

"Since you will not live to tell my little secret, I confess. I killed my way to the top. Made to look like unfortunate accidents. When the disk is retrieved from Dragonfly, Corsair Enterprises will disappear again."

"Hazel knows," Mark said bitterly. "She won't keep that kind of secret for long."

"That sow thinks she has permanent possession of my diamonds. When I meet her again, I will see to it that she returns them all and then her mouth will be sealed permanently."

"Then she was not working for you?"

"Working for me?" Laughing evilly he boasted, "She thinks she can outsmart me, the man that has deceived an entire military establishment for all these years." Casually, he tossed a stone over the edge and waited for the sound it would make. "I would advise you to stay away from the edge. It almost caved in with me once. Even a sudden noise can cause the sand to shift and give way." Dropping another stone into the dark hole, he listened. Ten seconds later the sound of the hollow splash resounded back up the shaft. "Your tiny ledge is where I was first confined when the slave driver's son brought me here. Soon you will experience true darkness."

Then he quickly walked back up the tunnel. Mark watched the light reflecting on the walls and ceiling until it was gone. Suddenly it was very, very dark.

CHAPTER TWENTY-FIVE

The stretch limo passed through the iron gates following the serpentine driveway to the road. At the entrance, the don said through the glass partition that separated them, "When we rounded that last curve, something metallic reflected back from the headlights. See what it is."

Through the window, the mafia soldier shinned the flashlight toward a clump of bushes. "It's a car, boss."

"What are you waiting for? Investigate."

Walking over, he turned the light into the rental car. Betty Ann crouched below the window. He opened the door and grabbed her by the arm, picked her up he placed her on his shoulder like a sack of flower. At the limo, he dropped her to the ground. "It's the broad from the tower, boss. What you want I should do?"

"Well, so it is. Bring her to me. I would have a word with her." Handing him the rent-a-car key, the soldier pushed Betty Ann roughly into the back seat and the don pulled her tight against his body. "My lucky day indeed. Now you will tell me where your companions are hiding their computer."

"Fat chance," she said, squirming, trying to pull loose.

"Calm yourself, my dear. You will do this small favor for me." Suddenly, he held a knife in his hand. The sharp pointed blade gleamed ominously. "Would you like to see the damage my little war trophy can do to those pretty brown eyes? It is very sharp."

"Don't!" she squealed. Catching him off guard, she broke loose and scooted over against the far side and cowered against the window.

"Oh, I do hope you won't force me to use this," he said, turning the blade back and forth. It flashed ominously. "Once done, you will never see another sunset, never watch a puppy fetch a stick, never see a kitten play with a ball of yarn." Suddenly, he pounced on her and brought the point close to her eye. Screaming, Betty Ann turned her head away. "You have five seconds to make up your mind."

The point came closer and she could see the swastika etched on the side. "Oh God," she moaned.

Suddenly, the door opened beside her and the mafia soldier grabbed her roughly. "Hold her head steady. I haven't done this for some time. The juice from the eye ball always drips on everything."

"All right," she panted. "I'll tell you, I'll tell you!"

At the house in Wingate, the lights were off and all was dark. With Betty Ann locked in the back seat, the don and the soldier slipped in through the kitchen door. Walpole was asleep when the knifepoint prodded his neck and he suddenly awoke. The don put a hand over his mouth and whispered, "Who else is in the house?"

"How should I know dat? I been sleepin'."

The soldier came in and turned on a light. "Nobody else here, boss."

The don pulled Walpole to his feet. "You will come with me little man."

"Do I got a choice?"

"Not if you wish to live."

"Yeah, dat's what I figured." Offering no resistance, he went with them to the computer room. In a few minutes the disassembled machine was in the trunk and they drove away with Betty Ann and Walpole locked in the back seat.

Betty Ann whispered, "He's taken Ted and Mark to some place out in the country."

"Day still alive?"

"I don't know," she whispered. "He forced me to tell him about our house. I didn't want to."

"And you was afraid I'd tell. Dat figures."

"What can we do?"

"Beats me. We gotta tink of somethin' though."

From the front seat, the don said, "Soon, you will have a last reunion with your friends." He bragged, "It took quite some time and no small effort, but finally I will have accomplished my goal. You will all be together under one roof, so to speak."

Betty Ann heard the coldness in his voice. "Where are they?"

He chortled merrily. "As with them, I must keep you in the dark on that subject."

Walpole rolled his eyes. "Dat don't sound good."

"Very perceptive of you, little man."

Walpole pleaded through the glass partition, "Come on, how 'bout lettin' me out. I'll keep my mouth shut, okay?"

Like a cat playing with a mouse, the mafia chieftain chuckled, "No, no, there is much news for you to catch up on. You mustn't miss out on all the games I have planned."

"Sheesh, ya got what ya came for, da kid and da big guy and da broad here. You don't need me no more."

He looked over his shoulder and chortled. "If you leave now you'll miss the fun."

"Dat's okay, I can't stay for no drawin'."

"But what about your reunion?" the don said. "Your friends will be there. They'll all be so *hurt*." He shrieked with laughter at his joke.

Walpole whispered to Betty Ann, "I don't like da way he said dat."

"Now that my electricity is back on again," he continued, "your computer will be useful."

As the limo drove away from the Wingate house, a phone in the hotel room in Monroe began to ring. The figure stationed at the window picked it up. "Yes?"

After a pause, he said, "My hunch was right, then." He stood silently, listening to the person on the other end. Dropping his lit cigarette on the floor, he put it out with his shoe. "The stakeout in Wingate paid off! Well, don't loose the limo this time." Quietly, he placed the receiver back on its cradle.

CHAPTER TWENTY-SIX

Back in the mine, Mark whispered, "I've never been any place so dark before. I hate this." His voice bounced off the wall in front of him and came back sounding louder than he expected. "Feel like I'm gonna slide into that pit."

"Still alive aren't you? Come toward the sound of my voice."

There's an echo. I can't tell where your voice is coming from."

"Hell, Mark, do something."

Mark moved a hand out and felt the sand begin to move under it. Quickly, he pulled it back. "Oh God, I can't breathe!"

"Just come to me, Mark. You'll be okay."

His voice sounding miserable, Mark said, "But I turned some after it got dark. I don't know."

"Damn-it, follow the sound of my voice."

"But the echo."

Ted put his hand out, intending to grab him and pull him away from the edge. Then he felt something lodged in the sand. "There's something here."

"Oh hell, what, Ted?"

"Piece of cloth, a shirt maybe."

Mark's trembling voice rose another octave. Emphasizing each word, he said slowly, "I want you to know, Ted. It does not make me feel any better to know that someone else was down here."

"Just a shirt."

"Are there any bones? Maybe somebody died."

"No bones."

"Oh God, whoever left it, fell down the hole, Ted."

"Or escaped across it."

"Or tried to, and fell in!" Hyperventilating, Mark began to pant, "Can't you see? We're gonna die."

"Calm down, Mark. I'll come get you."

"No, Ted," he wailed, "You'll push us both over the edge."

Ted tried to keep his voice calm. "I caught a glimpse of a ledge by the hole. Maybe we can crawl back across."

"Are you crazy! You heard that maniac! He said the dirt would crumble even from a loud noise."

"So keep your voice down." Ted's hand found Mark and he pulled him forward and placed him against the wall. "I've got to do this," he said, as he crept forward on hands and knees.

"What?" Mark whimpered. "I can't see in the dark."

At the shaft, Ted slid his hand out along the ledge. Suddenly he could feel the earth sliding out from under him and he heard, far below, the sound of gravel splashing into water. Propelling himself backward away from the edge, ensnared in the tugging current of sand, he fought his way back to firm ground and lay panting against Mark.

Mark hugged the wall and listened to his heavy breathing, "Was that a cave in? I told you it would. I told you!"

"Shut up, let me think." Ted felt around again with his free hand. The sand was still moving, but not like it had been before. "The edge is unstable."

"Maybe the General will come back."

"Yeah, to watch us die."

"Don't say that, Ted."

"He has to make sure I'm really dead."

"I don't want to die, Ted!"

"Then, we better get out before he comes back."

"How can we do that? How? Even if that board was still across the hole, in the dark, we'd never make it."

Suddenly, Ted remembered the matchbook he had dropped into his shirt pocket back at Mom's Diner. Suddenly, the match flared, looking as bright to Mark as a headlight on a freight train. "You had matches all along?"

"From the diner." Ted grinned as he held it up. "I'd forgotten about 'em." In the brief period that the match stayed lit, they saw the dark gaping maw, ten feet across, directly in front of them.

"God, Ted, look at that!"

"Yeah, too far to jump." On the other side, the long board protruded out two feet over the edge toward them.

"Can you reach it, Ted?" The match went out and Mark groaned as the terrible blackness enveloped them again.

Ted found Mark's hand in the dark and put the matchbook into it. "Keep the matches lit, one at a time."

Mark's hand trembled as he struck the first match. Ted lay on his stomach and with the shirt he lassoed a nail extending from the end of the board. "Hold my legs. Don't let me fall." He began to drag the board toward him across the deep void. "You're doing it, Ted!"

Twenty-minutes later, back at the farmhouse, the general and his accomplice hustled Betty Ann and Walpole into the front room and locked them in a closet. Outside in the dark, Ted and Mark watched through a window as the don quickly set up the computer and started typing. "That's your computer, Ted. He's after the files."

"Find a phone; call the police. I've got to stop him before he gets away."

"You've been avoiding cops ever since I met you. You sure you want cops?"

"When the General's caught, I'll be off the hook."

"I don't get it."

"He's still alive, Mark. That's proof I didn't kill him."

"Okay, I'll try, but what about the rest of his gang? They're out there someplace."

"There's a house about a mile back. Saw a light on."

"Can't we both go?"

"I'm not letting him out of my sight. Hurry!" Mark took off down the road at a trot and Ted found an old oak tree with a gnarled limb hanging out over the back porch roof. Shinnying along the branch, he dropped quietly onto the roof. Slipping through a second floor window, he tiptoed over the squeaky floor out onto a hallway landing. At the stairwell railing, he listened to fragments of the conversation drifted up from the floor below.

The General's voice sounded angry. "She wants me to meet her at the Klondike Diner tomorrow at ten. The audaciousness of this fat sow! She even knows my business address. She's sent an e-mail to Corsair Enterprises professing to know where Dragonfly is. And that *he* has the disk! For more diamonds, this woman will give him to me! Can you believe that?"

"What you want I should do, boss?"

"The fool! She is not aware that her message has been traced to its source. It originated from an apartment building at 200 Spring Street."

"Where's that boss?"

"In Charlotte, near that Mom's Diner!"

"I'll take care of her, boss."

"No. After I dispose of the two in the closet, we will both go there and confront this insolent sow. When I get my hands on her, she will plead to give us this Dragonfly person."

Ted leaned out over a stairwell railing for a better look. Suddenly, he felt the banister giving way. Before he could pull back, it broke and he felt himself falling toward the floor below.

CHAPTER TWENTY-SEVEN

At the gate Mark noticed a dim light off in the underbrush. He approached closer. *That's the Rent-a-car!* Entering it, he sat behind the wheel. *No keys!* Just then an automobile pulled up to the entrance, parked, and the headlights were extinguished. Mark quickly closed his door and the interior light went off. He watched as three men got out and started walking down the driveway toward the farmhouse; one carrying a flashlight. *More hoods?* Waiting until they were out of sight, he popped the trunk and removed the machine pistol. Quietly, he followed them along the curved driveway.

On the front lawn of the farmhouse, the three men huddled. Then one separated from the others and stepped up onto the porch. He was tall. His angular face, worn with age, was framed by scraggly gray hair. Pushing open the front door, he burst into the room with a small caliber pistol held in his hand. In a stage voice worthy of a larger audience, he said dramatically, "General Fitzhammer, I presume."

The don, caught leaning over Ted on the floor, whirled around. His eyes wide, he hissed, "*You!*"

The old man smiled as his shaggy eyebrows knitted. "I see you still have a propensity for handguns. Please drop it." Without hesitation, the General released the pistol that he had been holding and clasp his hands behind his neck. The General, avoiding his subordinate's surprised stare, said, "You were always a Lone Ranger, Alexius."

Pointing at the subordinate, Wickersham ordered, "You, on the floor, face down."

Watching his subordinate hit the floor, the General continued, "Still too proud to bring a backup, I see. Not many of your ilk left, Alexius. I assumed you were long dead."

Running slender translucent fingers through thinning locks, the old man replied triumphantly, "And I was convinced that you were not. I located the surgeon that altered your face. Too bad those Venezuelan doctors keep no photographs of their work. My search would have been made easier."

Arrogantly, the General turned his head to one side. "A perfect profile, don't you think?"

"More distinguished than the button nose you started out with."

The General's restless blue eyes suddenly narrowed. "I don't suppose you'd consider some small offer of appeasement? Possibly, in the form of precious gem-stones?"

"You know there is more to my game than mere remuneration. When rich villains have need of poor ones, poor ones may make what price they will."

"Still spouting from the bard? Your manner of speech was always eloquent. Your Shakespearean guise worked so well. It threw off cohorts on both sides."

"Very flattering. Beware of flattery; it corrupts both the receiver and the giver."

The General's cold eyes narrowed. "MI-5 doesn't pay much. You know there's a great deal wealth to be had."

"No largess will quench my thirst to prove my point to the young bloods at home office."

Noticing a tremor in Wicherham's hand, he smiled. "You could live like a czar in the few years you have left."

"Too long the play to trade now for rubles. Truth will finally out and the world will know you still walk among the living."

Imperceptibly, the General loosened the grip on his fingers. "How did you find me?"

"By watching our Sergeant Wielding, of course. We knew he would find you - or you him." Taking pleasure in his victory, the old thespian said with great self-satisfaction, "The surprise was discovering that the mysterious mafia don and you were one and the same. How did that novelty come about, pray tell?"

"With the diamonds, of course. Do the Americans know you are here?"

Ted groaned and Alexius Wickersham glanced in his direction, then quickly returned his watery eyes back on the General. "No. The yanks would have demanded to know the why of it."

His hands still clasped together, the General looked down at Ted. "And you would have had to tell them about staking him out."

Wickersham chortled, "Precisely. If they had been aware, they would have pounced immediately." The self-satisfied note in the old man's voice was unmistakable. "We would have lost our bait, and you would have remained invisible."

"So we both used him."

The wintry old warrior glanced in Ted's direction again. "While under this man's roof, I discovered him to be an innocent. Ensnared by your craving for riches."

The General's eyes flashed. "And what is wrong with a hunger for wealth?"

Wickersham's eyebrows lowered. "At times we all lust for such largesse, old boy, but there are degrees of desperation." Leaning over Ted, while watching the General closely, he felt his neck for a pulse. Then he stood again. In the old days you were heroic helping the underground resistance. Flying in supplies and flying out downed pilots. I would never have thought of you as such a greedy type. "

"Or such a rogue?" The General continued wistfully, "In my youth, all I craved was freedom from that damned mine. Then later it became clear to me that extreme wealth is the only true freedom."

The old man shook his head sadly. "When you flew me out of occupied France that time, I thought you a selfless hero."

"That part of my life is over, Alexius, as is yours. Making me a General for those deeds was not enough. I required money. A great deal of money."

"And you killed to obtain it."

"But also, to keep my secret safe."

Ted moaned and his eyes fluttered open. Alexius glanced down. In one quick motion, the General slid his dagger from the sheath hidden inside his shirt behind his neck and plunged it into the old thespian's throat. Twisting the pistol from his hand, he said coldly, "It's still safe."

Ted saw the quick thrust and tried to rise. As he struggled to his feet, the bullet from the British agent's pistol, now in the hand of the General, hit him in the chest. It propelled him back against the wall. An expression of surprise on his face, he slowly collapsed to the floor.

In one quick motion, as the other two agents rushed in, the General fired his pistol. The first agent fell, a bullet in his head. The second agent fired as Fitzhammer stepped behind his subordinate and the mafia soldier died instantly. General Fitzhammer fired again hitting the second agent in the heart.

His blood up, he hissed, "Now the two in the closet. Wild eyed, he ran to the closet door and pulled on it. It was bolted from the inside. "You can't escape," he yelled. Standing back, he pointed the pistol at the door, deciding where the first shot should be placed. "You must die!"

Through the window, Mark watched in horror as the mad man stood between him and the closet door, his pistol raised. *Can't shoot. Betty Ann's in the closet.* To distract, Mark fired the machine pistol into the air.

The General instantly dropped to the floor. Abandoning the closet, he scampered on hands and knees into the kitchen. "I'm surrounded!" he shrieked. Pulling open a trap door in the floor, he slipped into the root cellar.

Mark burst through the front entrance just in time to see the trap door slam shut. Seeing Ted on the floor, rage overcame fear. Raising the trapdoor enough to thrust the pistol barrel through, he fired into the darkness below. When there was no response, he opened it and followed after this man that had just killed his friend.

The General was no where in sight. Ready to fire at the slightest movement, he ran into the mine a few yards. Then he stopped and listened, the only sound, the pounding of his heart. Quickly, he ran back into the root cellar and poked his head out into the night. Crickets were chirping and somewhere in the distance a whip-poor-will called. The General had vanished.

Then he heard it, the distant sound of pounding. *Betty Ann?* He cautiously hurried around the house and rushed back into the living room. The sweet pungent odor of gun smoke and blood sickened him as he ran to the closet door. "Betty Ann?" he yelled.

"Mark?"

"Yeah. It's me."

"There's a catch on your side beneath the knob." He found it and she tumbled out. "I heard shots?"

Walpole following her out, looked around apprehensively. "Look at all da dead guys!" Then he saw Ted's crumpled body. "Is dat Ted?"

Mark nodded, his lower lip began to quiver. "He's dead."

"No," Betty Ann wailed. "He can't be." She ran to him. Falling on her knees beside him she propped his head in her lap. "Oh Ted, speak to me. Speak to me."

"What happened, Mark?" Walpole asked.

Mark wiped tears from his eyes with the palm of his hand. "The General shot him."

Betty Ann pulled Ted's body to her tightly and rocked him back and forth. "No, no, she moaned. Mark's words began to sink in. "The General! Was he here too?"

"You saw him, Betty Ann. The don *is* the General."

"But Ted would have recognized him."

"His face had been altered with surgery."

Betty Ann put her cheek against Ted's head and whispered, "Oh God, please don't be dead."

Suddenly, Ted's eyes fluttered open, and he groaned. "What happened?"

"You're alive!" Betty Ann pushed him away and his head hit the floor. "Ted Lowen, don't you ever do that to me again!" Grabbing him up again, she hugged him to her breast. "You scared me half to death!"

"What happened," he asked again, sitting up and feeling his chest. Reaching into his shirt pocket he pulled out his billfold. "This thing saved me. Look at it." The leather wallet, stuffed with papers and money, had a dent in it where the bullet had bounced off. "Bullet knocked the breath out of me."

Betty Ann wiped her eyes and helped him to his feet. Suddenly she saw Wickersham's body crumpled in the corner. "Mercy! How did he get here?" She knelt beside him. "He was the sweetest man."

Sadly, Mark said, "He came here with those other two."

"And the don, I mean the General killed them all?"

Mark nodded. "He's a dead shot and really quick with that knife."

Walpole stared at the dagger, still in Wickersham's throat. "Yeah, he sure was partial to it."

"Wish I could have saved him." Mark's eyes began to fill with tears again as he looked down at the old thespian. Betty Ann put her arm around his shoulder. "Mark, you saved us all. The General would have killed everyone if you hadn't stopped him."

Ted began to revive. "Where is he, anyway?"

"He got away, Ted." Apologetically, Mark looked from Ted to Betty Ann. "I followed him into the mine. He's somewhere in there, I think."

Ted picked up the machine pistol. "No matter," he said. "I know where to find him."

"How could you know that, Ted?"

"He's after Hazel, Mark." Ted started for the door. "Before I fell, I heard him tell the guard."

"What are you going to do, Ted?"

"Go after him, Betty Ann."

"Oh, Ted, please. Let's just all go home. He's too dangerous."

"Gotta end it now, or I can never stop running." He stepped out onto the porch and turned back. "Go home and wait for me there. Take the kid and Walpole. Mark looks beat."

Betty Ann ran after him, but he had already vanished into the night. "We'll be waiting, Ted," she called out. There was no reply.

CHAPTER TWENTY-EIGHT

At the rental car, the General tucked the small pistol in his sock and pulled his pants leg down over it. Then he put the larger one in his coat pocket. *Now, to deal with that fat pig.*

It was two o'clock in the morning when he pulled up in front of the rundown tenement house on Spring Street. Finding a parking place under a large water oak that gave him a view of both the front and side of the building, he sat and watched the darkened windows. A man, dressed in ragged denims, leaned on a phone booth near the entrance. He looked up and down the street anxiously, as he safeguarded a thin woman in a worn sweat suit while she talked on the phone. When she hung up, together, they hurried back into the apartment building.

Inside apartment number seven Hazel stood at a window in the darkened room, watching the street through a lifted corner of the closed shade. Harry, stretched out on the bed, was cleaning his fingernails with a penknife. "Harry, a car drove up and parked in that space under the tree."

"What you think them spaces is out there for, Hazel?"

"Don't be such a wise ass. Nobody got out and it's been at least ten minutes now."

Rolling over onto his side, he grinned and propped his head up on his elbow. "So, some kid is gettin' some."

"Don't think so, Harry. It's too new for this neighborhood. When do you remember seeing any of the sweet young things around here out with somebody with money? Wait, someone's getting out. It's that guy, Harry!"

"Who?"

"The one I took the diamonds off of. He just went around to the front!"

Harry bounced out of bed and peered out over Hazel's shoulder. "He sure found us in a hurry."

"It was the tracer program. That Mark kid told Dragonfly, remember?"

Harry sat back on the bed, and smirked. "That do-dad led him right to us."

"That was the plan, wasn't it?" She kept watching. "That's why I've been staring out this window all night, don't you think?"

"Well, I'm ready for him." Harry jumped up and pulled his pistol from the leather holster and pranced nervously around the room. "Just let him in. I'll be in the closet with this thing."

"Wait, now he's getting back in his car."

"And driving off?"

"No, just sitting there."

Suddenly, an ancient alarm bell in the back of the building began to clang. "The fire alarm!" Harry said. "This old heap will go up like a grease fire." He went to the window and stood beside Hazel, watching as the street began to fill with people waiting for the fire trucks to arrive.

"I don't smell smoke; do you?"

"Don't mean nothin', Hazel. We'd best get out while we can."

Two teenage boys were perched on the hood of the new car parked under the tree. "He wouldn't let those kids sit there, Harry. That guy ain't in his car anymore!"

Harry pulled the shade up higher. "Can't see him in the crowd?"

"He's trying to smoke us out, Harry. Just like them boys at the office the other day. Didn't go for it then and I ain't falling for it now! He's trying to get us out in the open."

"I'll go out the front, Hazel; you take the back. He can't watch both doors."

She picked up the bag of diamonds. "I'm not leaving these, Harry."

He checked his pistol one more time. "Stuff 'em in your bra. It'll take him a week to find 'em there."

"Hell, that's the first place he'd try," she snickered. "You better take half, just in case."

He chuckled as he put his share of the diamonds in his pocket and opened the door just enough to peep out into the hall. "It's clear. Remember our fallback plan. Wait for me there." Slipping out into the hallway, Hazel followed. Hazel muttered to the door she was closing, "You always got one, don't you." People were running, carrying suitcases, clothes hampers, and what ever they could find to put their belongings into. When a panicked couple rushed past her, Hazel followed behind them through the back door under the clanging bell. Once outside, she made a dash for an outbuilding behind the tenement. The don, waiting in the shadows, watched her slip into the shed.

The one room outbuilding, with slatted vertical plank walls, smelled of stale trunks and empty crates. Through the open spaces between the boards, a street light in the next block cast jagged streaks of light across the jumble of rubbish accumulated in the cramped chamber. Hazel quickly found her way across the dirt floor to the back and unlocked a second door. Then she came back to the front and hid in a dark corner behind a crate.

Suddenly, the front door opened, and the General stepped inside. He held a pistol in his hand. In a quiet voice, he said, "I know you're in here." As he peered into the room, his eyes not yet accustomed to the darker surroundings, Hazel backed deeper into the shadows. Suddenly, her elbow raked against something. It fell to the floor with a thud. In a sing song voice, he whispered, "Come out, come out, where ever you are."

Stepping from behind the box, Hazel glared defiantly at him.

"The appointment wasn't until tomorrow, Big Shot."

"You have something of mine."

"You're way too early."

He took a step closer. "Also, it is time for you to produce this Dragonfly person."

"Well, he won't be here 'till tomorrow."

"Matters have suddenly become urgent. It must be tonight ... if you want more of my diamonds."

"Forget it, Big Shot. I told you, you're way too early."

"Then you will give back all the diamonds." He moved closer.

Hazel folded her arms across her chest, and glared at him. "We had a deal. I kept my end of it."

Suddenly, he was standing in front of her, so close that she could smell his breath. "Well, the deal has become null and void." He nudged her with the pistol. "As you will be also, if you do not produce Dragonfly without delay."

"I told you sport, he won't be here 'till tomorrow." Angrily, he raised his hand to slap her; she stepped back. Light from outside abruptly fell across her face. "Wouldn't do that. You might get yourself shot up a little." She was grinning.

Suddenly, he sensed another person in the room. As he raised his weapon, Harry suddenly pressed his pistol into the small of the surprised man's back. Hazel laughed, "Bet his is bigger than yours."

Leaning around the general, Harry relieved him of his weapon. "See if he has the rest of 'em, Hazel."

Angrily, the gangster locked his fingers behind his head. "This is the second time you've tricked me. You will live to regret it."

Hazel patted his vest, feeling for a bulge. "Don't take it so hard, Big Shot. We're just smarter than you, that's all." She found the little bag right where she had seen him place it, the night before. "We got 'em, Harry!"

"Now what, Hazel?"

"We do like you said, before, Harry. We get the hell out of Dodge, this time for good." She held the leather bag up by its drawstrings and shook it in Harry's face. "We're gonna live like kings."

Harry produced a rope and began to tie the General's wrists together. "What about Moon and Avis?" he said.

"What about 'em? We don't need 'em, do we?"

"But you told Avis about the sparklers. They'll be expecting a cut."

She laughed. "I'll send 'em a post card, with an apology."

With the General's hands secured, Harry threw the rope's end over a ceiling beam. "Well, what about this one, then?"

"Leave 'em."

The General stood with his hands stretched above his head, looking uncomfortable. Harry glanced at Hazel and grinned, then pulled hard on the rope and secured it. "That's not too tight, is it, your majesty? Don't want a person of your stature and breeding to feel too humiliated."

The General glared at them. "Possibly, you are not aware that the officials are hot on my heels. They know about the diamonds and will certainly wish to return them to their rightful owners."

"He's got a point, Hazel."

"Forget it, Harry. They're after him, not us."

The General's toes barely touched the floor, as he hung helplessly from the rafter. "It would be wise to allow me to remain at large."

"What you think, Hazel? If he talks, they'll come after us. They'll take 'em back, for sure."

"Not if they can't find 'em, Harry." Hazel reached into her bra and removed a package containing her half of the diamonds. She dropped it into the leather bag she had just liberated from the underworld leader. "Give me yours, Harry." He handed his half over and she put them in with the others. Poking the irate man in the stomach with her finger, she said. "Thanks for the warning, sport. These will be hid way before they ever cut you down."

"Those were my last!" He began to struggle, straining at the ropes binding him. "I will hound you until you die."

Hazel grinned at Harry, ignoring his ranting. "I'll put these in a safe place. Know where I mean?"

"Where you used to hide stuff when you was a kid?"

"Yeah. They'll be safe there 'til we're ready for 'em. Even if they found our new safe house and stuck us in jail, these little beauties will be waiting when we get out. And only you and I know where the hidey-hole is, right?"

"I ain't gonna tell, if you ain't. See you at the safe house, Hazel?"

"Yeah, tomorrow night, then, before long, it's off to see the wizard."

"Yeah, the wonderful wizard."

CHAPTER TWENTY-NINE

Ted drove the limo slowly along Spring Street. People milled about on the sidewalk, watching firemen rolling up fire hoses after the false alarm. Suddenly, in the glare of the fire truck's flashing red light, he saw the rent-a-car parked under the big water oak. Hazel was hastily loading suitcases into the back. Ted pulled the limo in behind her. Stepping out of the car, he growled, "Where's the man that came in this car?"

Defiantly, Hazel turned and folded her arms across her chest. "What are you talking about, hot shot? This is my car."

"Yeah, like the one I'm driving ain't stolen either."

Hazel glanced at the black auto, then at the pistol in his hand. "Who'd you steal yours from?"

"A couple of dead guys. You could be next. Where is he?"

"I told you, it's mine."

"Don't lie to me. This is my rent-a-car. I know the tag number."

"Okay, so I'm borrowing it. I thought it was his."

"Where's the man that came in it?"

"Do I look like an information booth?"

"I'm in no mood to play games, woman." Ted jabbed the pistol into her midsection. "I don't have time for this!"

She grunted, and took a quick breath. "Easy with that thing. I'll tell you, but you gotta let me leave before you talk to him."

Ted's eyes narrowed. "How do I know you ain't lying?"

"He's close by, I swear, and he sure as hell ain't going nowhere."

"So where the hell is he?"

"Real close." Ted noticed that her attitude suddenly was no longer confrontational. "Look, I'll level with you. There's some passports and stuff I have to pick up. I need 'em in a hurry."

"So?"

"They're in Monroe." She pulled the suitcase that she had been loading out of the rent-a-car. "You take your car; the keys are in the ignition. I'll drive the black one. Deal?"

Ted quickly opened the driver's side door and checked. "Okay, Deal. Now where is he?"

She pointed over her shoulder with her thumb. "In that out building back there." Ted started to leave. "No need to rush, sport. He's all tied up, so to speak."

"What's that mean?"

"Means he's tied up, you'll see." She began hastily placing her bags in the limo. "Tell him Hazel said hello."

At that moment behind the apartment building, an angry fire marshal, his big face matching the color of his fire truck, was questioning a tenant about who might have turned in the false alarm. Behind them, he noticed a figure come out of the out building and rush away. Suspiciously, he opened the door to the shed and shined his light onto the General hanging by his wrists from the cross beam. Rushing over, he pulled the gag from his mouth. "What's going on here?"

"Cut me down."

"What happened?"

"The man that turned in that false alarm just left. I caught him in the act and he forced me in here and tied me up."

The fireman reached up and started untying the rope. "Why would he do that?"

"So that he could escape, you idiot! Cut me down!"

Before he could untie the rope, Ted walked through the door. Seeing what was happening, he quickly tucked the machine pistol into his belt and pulled his shirt over it. "Don't let that man go. He's a war criminal!"

The big fireman turned around. "Who are you?"

"He just murdered three people. Don't untie him."

Behind the fireman's back, the General struggled with the ropes still tied around his wrists. He blurted out; "Do you see any dead bodies? He's lying to save himself."

"Back in Wingate, not here," Ted stammered. "On his farm."

"This is the man that tied me up, Marshal. He'll say anything to get out of this. Look at my clothes. Do farmers wear business suits? Draw your own conclusions, man!"

The marshal scratched his head, looking perplexed. "Why don't you both come with me. We'll sort this out down at the station house."

"Splendid idea," the General said. "Just untie me; then we'll call the Wingate authorities. They'll confirm that there are no dead bodies."

"This is General Fitzhammer, damn-it." Ted's voice began to rise. "He is a war criminal!"

"The man is lying, Marshal. I can prove who I am. He is the war criminal, not I."

The overweight fire marshal turned back to the General and began again to release his wrists from the rope. "I'll get to the bottom of this at the station house."

"Don't untie him!" Ted's voice sounded harsh and threatening in the small building. "He's already killed several times tonight. Let him go and he'll do it again." No longer sure of what to do, the befuddled man stopped again. "There's a policeman out front. Maybe ..."

The General interrupted, his vice becoming hysterical. "Don't listen to him, marshal! He wants you to keep me this way so he can attack you without my interference. Look, he has a weapon in his belt."

The fireman glanced over his shoulder back at Ted. The outline of the pistol beneath it was hard to miss. Suddenly, the fire marshal made up his mind. He turned and held out his hand. "We'll sort this out at the station house. Give me that weapon."

"Not until this man is behind bars!" Ted reached for the pistol. It was halfway out, when the big marshal grabbed his hand. Pinning the gun against his side, the heavy man wrestled Ted to the ground. Over the fireman's shoulder, Ted watched helplessly as the General quickly finished untying his bonds.

Slowly he removed the pistol from his sock. "Hazel has my diamonds, and I left you for dead." Taking careful aim at Ted's face, he snarled, "This time you'll stay dead."

Ted rolled, just as the weapon fired and the bullet entered the fireman's heart. The marshal's hand relaxed and the machine pistol came free. The second bullet hit inches from Ted's head as he rolled again and fired. Three pinholes of light appeared in the tin roof to the left of the General's head, just before he turned and fled out into the night.

Trapped beneath the fireman's dead weight, Ted watched through the open door as his old enemy entered the rent-a-car and drove away. The gunfire had been heard. Seconds seemed like hours, as Ted struggled out from under the fireman's body. A policeman rushed into the building just as Ted slipped, unseen, out through the back door.

CHAPTER THIRTY

An hour later, hiding in the shadows of Mom's Diner, Ted saw Matilda, as Betty Ann drove underneath the streetlight and pulled to the curb. Mark and Walpole were in the back. Ted squeezed in and ducked down low in the seat. "Get us out of town fast."

"Must be a dozen patrol cars on Spring Street, Ted. What happened? Did you find the General?"

"Yeah, but he got away again. He let slip that Hazel stole his diamonds. They must be worth close to a million."

Walpole muttered. "She's gotta be rich now."

Ted nodded. "That's why she was in such a hurry."

"The General told you all this?"

"Yeah, Betty Ann. Somehow, Hazel had the General all tied up, when I found him."

"Tied up?"

"Long story. Still can't prove he's alive." Ted ducked lower, as a squad car passed by.

"It's okay," Walpole said, craning his neck, "It's gone."

Ted raised up and looked back at the departing cruiser resting his hand on the front seat beside Betty Ann. "Every time, I think I have him, he manages to kill off my witness."

"And keep his secret safe."

"Not all together, Mark. Now Hazel knows."

Walpole piped up, "Den we has to get Hazel to rat to da law!"

"Not that simple. She's skipping town."

"We've all seen him, Ted. They'll have to believe us now."

"Don't count on it, Betty Ann." Ted looked morosely out the window as they sped by Sweet Union Flea Market. "Won't be another trial."

Betty Ann sighed, "Guess Mark could try contacting Dragonfly again. He might still know how to get in touch with her."

"Computer's at that farmhouse."

"No it ain't," Walpole piped up again. "Its back in Wingate already. We did a rescue job on it 'fore we split."

Betty Ann reached out and took Ted's hand. "I'm worried, Ted. The General knows where we live, now."

"Don't worry; he's got his hands full."

"How is that?"

"After I called you, I placed another call to the police." He smirked, "Told 'em I saw him kill a fireman tonight."

"He killed again?"

"Yeah Betty Ann, he's in our rent-a-car. He'll be keeping his head down for a while." Ted sat back and relaxed, turning the events over in his mind. Then a thought struck him. "How'd you get back to Wingate?"

"Mr. Walpole hiked out to 74 and hitched a ride. Drove Matilda back and picked us up." On the outskirts of Monroe, Betty Ann sped up to catch the green light at hilltop, and raced down the hill toward the bridge. "I was scared to death that more of the don's, I mean the General's, men would come before we could get away."

"Anyone show?"

"No. We waited in the woods out of sight near the entrance. When Mr. Walpole came back with Matilda, we took a chance and went back for the computer." Betty Ann glanced back at Ted and chuckled. "At our house, I called the Monroe police and told 'em I'd heard a lot of gun-fire in the woods. Didn't give my name."

In the distance the Wingate tower came into view. Suddenly a blue light began to flash and a siren growled. "Oh, mercy, Ted, what shall I do?"

"Pull over; you weren't speeding were you?"

"I wasn't paying attention. I may have." She brought Matilda to a stop on the side of the highway and a cruiser pulled in behind them.

The policeman came over to the driver's side and tapped on the window with his flashlight. Betty Ann rolled it down. "Why, Deputy Dutton! What ever are you doing out at this ungodly hour?"

He removed his smoky-the-bear hat with its gold colored lanyard and leaned his head in close to the open window. "Howdy, Ma'am. Is that you?"

Betty Ann smiled her prettiest smile. "Was I speeding? I surly hope not."

Grinning sheepishly, his wall-eye stared past her into the back seat. "Yes-um. You wuz when I seen you back at Hilltop." The blue flashing light cast an eerie pattern on his face, and he wheezed with each breath that he took. "You was a motorizin' right along as in if the end of the world was trying to catch you up."

"Oh my goodness, I guess you want to see my driver's license then."

"No ma'am. That's all right. I knows who you are." He shined the light into the back seat. "Don't guess this little vehicle will hole much more than you is hauling tonight. Kind of late to be out, ain't it?"

"We've been visiting my cousin up in Statesville. It got kind of late before we finished our visit."

"Yes-um. I knows how that is. My wife Avis is always doing that."

"You're out awful late yourself, deputy. When were you put on night duty?"

"Oh, I don't has to do this often, but they's been a big shoot-out over in the hollow. You know close to Shiner's Mountain." His face became grave, and his voice more solemn. "Some fellers got shot up some. Fact is, they all got their selves killed. Know what I mean?"

"Oh, mercy. How awful!"

"Yes-um. All us-inz is on duty tonight. Brung troopers all the way up from Wadesboro."

"Who in the world would have done such a thing?"

"Not exactly sure, but a fireman got his self blowed away in Charlotte tonight and they think it might be the same ones that done it here. Happened up at my sister's place."

"Your sister?"

"Yes-um. Well, not her place exactly, at the building where she was staying at. Hazel weren't in on it, though. Leastwise, not that I knows about. She won't answer her phone, so I can't tell for sure."

"Why, I'd be scared to death for her, deputy."

"Oh, she's all right, I guess." He straightened up, looking off into the distance. "They's a APB out for a tall man with blue eyes. Somebody said that he was the one that done it."

"Wasn't it a blue eyed man you mentioned the other day?"

"Oh, weren't him, ma'am. This-un was some sort of a General. The blue eyed man I seen was in a long black vehicle. General's mostly ride in little green jeeps. Anyways, that-un that I seen on the TV news did."

"He sounds like a dangerous man. If you see him, you better be careful."

Resting an arm on the roof, he leaned close to the window again. "Yes-um, I sure will. My sister told Avis that there was a tall blue eyed man that she was dickering with about something or other. Hope she's not got herself in a fix over it."

Mark leaned over between Betty Ann and Ted. "I'll bet it was about those diamonds! They must be worth millions." Walpole pulled Mark back, and nudged him with his elbow.

"Oh, don't be a ninny," Betty Ann said quickly. "This is entirely an unrelated matter."

Dutton leaned his head inside the window. "Did he say Diamonds?"

"Oh, that's just my house-guest, deputy," Betty Ann said, her words rushing out and running together. "He's young; has an overactive imagination, doesn't know what he's talking about." She smiled up at him appealingly. "Mercy, it's getting late. If you don't mind, I sure do need to get home to my warm little bed."

"Yes-um." He straightened up and stood beside the car, his wall-eye staring into the distance. Then he looked down and brushed something off the brim of his hat. "I'll be doing the same thing in about an hour. Shift changes at five." He put his hat back on. " Y'all have a nice night now, you hear? And keep down that motorizing. It ain't real safe."

Betty Ann quickly put Matilda in gear. "Thank you for the warning, Deputy Dutton. Nice to see you again." She smiled and waved as she hastily drove away. "Mark, don't *ever* tell that man anything that he doesn't already know," she said grimly. "He's slow as molasses runnin' up hill in the wintertime, but he's not quite as dumb as he acts."

"Sorry, Betty Ann. I wasn't thinking."

"He would keep us out here talking 'till the cows come home."

CHAPTER THIRTY-ONE

The next morning Mark sat in the living room watching the news on TV. A camera crew that had slipped past the police barricade was busily filming the grisly scene inside the farmhouse. "Betty Ann, Ted, come look at this!"

As she came in, the camera panned past two bodies sprawled on the floor, stopped on the body of Alexius Wickersham. Suddenly, the screen went black.

Betty Ann shuddered and sat down. "Poor Mr. Wickersham!" She wiped a tear from her cheek. "I hope they catch that killer soon. I'm sick and tired of this whole mess."

Mark's eyes looked large as he peered back at her through his horn-rimmed glasses. "Earlier, the newscaster announced he was a secret agent or a spy, something like that. And those other two had British passports on 'em."

"Spy? What do they know; he was just a sweet old man that liked to quote Shakespeare."

"Well they held up a leather packet with four passports in it. They all had different names but the same picture. It was Mr. Wickersham's face on all of them."

Sadly, Betty Ann shook her head and repeated, "Poor Mr. Wickersham."

Suddenly, the back door burst open and a man rushed through the kitchen and into the living room. His shiny black jumpsuit and thick body armor reflected back the blue light, suddenly flashing through the living room window. The short barreled weapon he was holding pointed directly at Ted. Simultaneously, the front door opened and three men dressed in the same fashion, charged in, each holding automatic weapons. Two more entered behind them and they spread out down the hallway, quickly searching the other rooms. Walpole, his eyes wide with fear, was herded into the living room, followed by one of the unit. Pressing a paper into Ted's hand, the leader said, "This is a search warrant. Are you Matthew J. Wielding?"

Ted glared back at him. "Who wants to know?"

"The US government."

He glanced at Betty Ann, then turned his face away. "It's almost a relief," he said, nodding to the squad leader. "Yeah, I'm him."

"You are under arrest for the murder of a General Fitzhammer."

Betty Ann stepped between the man with the paper and Ted, her fists clinched. "General Fitzhammer is not dead! We just saw him. Ted's not a murderer!"

"This warrant states that he has been convicted, ma'am, back in '45. Look, here is his wanted poster." He held it up so that she could read it. The picture on it was of a very young, but recognizable Ted in uniform.

Angrily, she snatched it from his hand. "This is a terrible lie! I tell you General Fitzhammer is not even dead. I spoke to him yesterday." She stamped her foot. "He was as alive as you are. I stood this close to him." She started to cry, tears streaming down her face. "Why can't you believe me?"

"Ma'am, you must have spoken to an impersonator."

"It *was* the General, I tell you. He even gloated about it to me." Suddenly, she saw Walpole standing in the hallway. "Mr. Walpole was there, he will tell you."

Walpole rolled his eyes. "She ain't lying. He's a real loony-tunes. He killed tree men at da farmhouse last night, right in front of us; was planning to kill us too. He's still alive and crazy as hell."

Betty Ann reached out and pulled at the swat team leader's sleeve. "You've got to believe us!"

An assistant placed handcuffs on Ted's wrists, as the apologetic leader gently removed Betty Ann's hand from his sleeve. "There will be a hearing tomorrow, ma'am. You can tell your story to a federal judge at that time. But let me warn you, the military moves swiftly on matters of this nature. Even if you had credible evidence, you may not have time to show it."

"Can't you do something?"

"My authority ends with his capture. Sorry, there's nothing else I can do."

Ted tested the cuffs restraining his wrists. "How'd you find me?"

"An anonymous phone tip."

Ted looked knowingly at Betty Ann. "Had to be the General."

"See?" Betty Ann said. "He's the only one that knew Ted was here."

"I saw him too," Mark said. "We all saw him. Why can't we make you believe us?"

Betty Ann began to cry again. "He's getting away with it. The general will go free and Ted will be executed." She reached for his sleeve again. "General Fitzhammer is alive; we *all* saw him!"

"It's out of my hands, now." Two of the team led Ted out onto the front porch. A crowd had collected around the police cruisers parked in the front yard. As the squad leader stood in the doorway, blocking Betty Ann from following, he said, "The hearing will be at the Union County courthouse in Monroe."

"What will happen to him?"

"He will be executed, of course."

"Without a trial?" Betty Ann wailed.

"There was a trial, ma'am. He has already been sentenced to be hanged."

"But he's innocent, I tell you. He didn't kill anyone!

Turning his back, the squad leader walked swiftly to the police cruiser and hustled Ted into the back seat. Then the procession drove slowly down Camden Street through the university campus. "Oh, Ted," Betty Ann whispered. "I've got to save you."

CHAPTER THIRTY-TWO

Back in Monroe at a ramshackle clapboard house near the railroad tracks, Harry burst through the back door of their latest safe house and walked quickly to the bedroom where Hazel was sleeping. "Wake up Hazel, it's already ten o'clock."

"Leave me be, Harry. It's been a long night. I need my beauty sleep."

"Thought you was gonna stash the sparklers in your secret hidey-hole."

"I did."

"The one under that bridge over the railroad tracks?"

"Yeah. Ain't no other one." She sat up in bed. "What's got in to you, Harry?"

"Well, I just came from over there, and they ain't in it."

"What are you talking about, you old fool. Sure they are. Put 'em there first thing, soon as I left that sucker tied up, last night."

Harry glared at her. "It was this morning, but, anyway I think I get the picture."

She swung her feet onto the floor and stood up. She was still dressed in the same clothes she had been wearing the night before. "What the hell does that mean, Harry?"

"You're planning on taking off without me; that's what it means."

"You been drinking?" She snatched a cigarette from a half-empty pack and lit up. "No way, Harry. We been together too long for that."

"Well, they is gone, Hazel, gone!"

Angrily blowing smoke through her nose, she said, "Nobody else knows about that place, Harry, except you and me. And that's where I left 'em." Suddenly, she turned on him. "This ain't nothing to joke about, Harry. You doing me around?"

"I ain't kidding, Hazel, they is gone, I tell you."

She glared at him. "Stop saying that! Let me think for a minute."

He stared back at her. "If you don't have 'em, and I ain't neither, then who does?"

She bit nervously on a hangnail. "There wasn't anybody else around, when I stashed 'em," She took another drag on her cigarette.

"Are you sure? I searched that there hole real good. I dumped out what was left of your pot and a half-empty bottle of Thunderbird, but there ain't no bag of diamonds."

"That other stuff's been in there since I was a kid, Harry. The bag was right on top of it. Sometimes bums sleep down there, but if there'd been one around last night, I'd of seen him."

"Well the stuff's gone. *Somebody* took it."

"Stop saying that! There's no place down there anyone could hide, without me seeing 'em. That's why I picked that spot when I was no more than twelve. So I could tell for sure that I was alone and wouldn't be seen." She dropped her cigarette and put a foot on it. "That sucker will be after us by now. Without the diamonds, we don't have enough money to get a hundred miles away."

Harry sat down on the bed and stared at his shoes. "There's nothing we can sell real quick that I can think of and I'm too damned old to start robbing banks. What you think, Hazel?"

She grimaced, frustration showing in her eyes. "I let it all slip right through my fingers, Harry. Those diamonds would have lasted us forever."

"Wait Hazel, didn't that message to Dragonfly that time, mention a thing that was worth big bucks. Something about breaking passwords?"

"Something like that, but who'd want to buy it?"

"And that company sure wanted to get that disk back."

"But that was the sucker's company."

"Well, with a company like that, he sure can't be broke. Maybe we can squeeze him again."

"What? We could get ourselves killed, Harry."

"Not if that feller Dragonfly gets into the act, Hazel."

Hazel thought about it for a minute. "Yeah, Harry, that might work."

As the swat team drove away with Ted handcuffed in the back seat, Betty Ann sat on the living room sofa dabbing tears with Mark's handkerchief. "They're going to execute him, Mark," she said. "Someone told them he was here."

Walpole looked uncomfortable. "Day just came out of nowheres while Mark was settin' da computer back up. After tomorrow, day'll haul his aa .. aa .. uh .. him off to some military prison. After dat, who knows what."

Mark sat down and put his arm around her shoulder. "Don't you worry, Betty Ann. We'll think of something."

Walpole rolled his eyes at Mark and sat down on the other side of her. "Fat chance. Couple of days ago, I was angling to find da soldier wit all dem jewels. Now it turns out Ted was da soldier all along, and now I'm angling to save his butt. Go figure."

"You're a different person now, Mr. Walpole." Betty Ann wiped her eyes again with the handkerchief. "We couldn't trust you then."

"You got dat right, lady. Funny how tings change."

"And people too," Mark said, glancing at Betty Ann, then he looked solemnly at Walpole. "If it makes you feel any better, I didn't know about Ted and the diamonds either."

"Yeah, well, guess I'm one of you guys now."

Betty Ann smiled through her tears. "And now we both need your help, Mr. Walpole."

He grinned at the irony. "If day had da General right in front of 'em, day'd have to believe us, wouldn't day?"

"He's changed his appearance," Betty Ann said.

"Can't change his fingerprints." Walpole slapped his hand on his knee. "Yeah, dat's what we gotta do."

Betty Ann studied Walpole's face for a second, then she said quietly, "Even if we knew where the General was, how could we ever capture him? Ted failed and he had the best chance of all."

"I agree with Walpole," Mark said. "We've got to do something."

The little detective scowled at Mark. "If da military had da General's fingerprints they'd have to turn Ted loose."

Walpole turned his face away, hiding his expression. "When I nailed dat guy at da college dat night, I wasn't sure I could do it, and he was just one person." Then he turned and looked back, a worried expression on his face. "Wonder how many more soldiers does he have, I mean guardin' him now? Might be an army for all we know."

"We must try something," Betty Ann said, sounding braver than she felt. "What would Ted do, if he were here?"

Mark started down the hallway. Over his shoulder he said, "Well I know what I'm gonna do. The feds think they got their man, and the British agents are all dead. It's up to me now."

Betty Ann whispered to Walpole, "He's so young."

"Yeah, but he's all we got."

As the hopelessness of the situation sank in, Betty Ann began to sob again. Walpole bit his lip, "Didn't mean dat stuff I said. We gonna tink of somethin', we got to."

A few minutes went by before Mark yelled out, "There's flash-mail!"

Betty Ann rushed into the computer room. "From Dragonfly?"

"No, from someone calling himself 'The Discoverer.'"

"What in the world?"

"Wants me to put him in touch with Hazel Dutton. He's heard that I might know where she can be found."

"Do you?"

"Of course not. I've already sent back that I don't have any idea where she is. Wait, there's another message coming in."

Walpole looked over Betty Ann's shoulder as they gazed into the glowing screen, her eyebrows knitted. "Maybe Dragonfly knows. They were in tight before."

"He says that a distant relative of hers died a while back and left her a large inheritance, but they didn't know where she had moved. He's been hired to find her and give her the news, but it has to be fast. The will has been contested and it will go to another party if she isn't found by next week. The other party claims that Hazel is dead. She's got to show herself to prove she's not."

"Ask him what's in it for us."

Mark frowned at Walpole. "I can't do that. Besides, if we can talk to Hazel she might know how to find the General."

"Well at least ask who this guy is."

They watched Mark hunched over the keyboard as he typed, his fingers moving quickly over the keys. "Where are you?"

"I'm in a nearby state. I can be in North Carolina by noon if you can contact Miss Dutton."

"Where can we meet?" Mark typed.

"You pick a suitable location, I'll meet you there."

"How about the Klondike?"

"Alaska?"

Betty Ann laughed as she watched Mark type, "No. It's the only restaurant in the town of Wingate, NC."

"Can you do this? Is it possible that you can locate Miss Dutton?"

"She was in this area yesterday. I may only be able to contact her through a third party on the net. I'll leave her a message to meet us there tonight for dinner. How will I know you?"

"I have her picture. I will know her. See you then."

Mark turned the swivel chair and faced Walpole and Betty Ann. "He signed off. I'll send Dragonfly an e-mail and see if he can get a message to Hazel. I'll invite him to come along too." Triumphantly, he said, What do you think now?"

"Mercy, that was so clever, Mark. If she shows up, we can ask her about the General."

"What if that *is* da General? Didn't Ted say somethin' like Hazel stole his merchandise?"

Betty Ann shuddered. "The general! What a terrible thought!"

"Come to think of it, he didn't ask what I looked like," Mark's young face looking grim, he said, "If it is him, I'm gonna be ready."

THIRTY-THREE

Hazel leaned over the sleeping form sprawled under a ragged patchwork quilt on the second-hand army cot. With a pudgy hand, she vigorously shook the musty bedspread. "Listen to this, Harry."

Harry opened his eyes and rolled off the bed, wiping sleep from his eyes. "I was sleeping, ya know."

"It's e-mail for Dragonfly."

"Hazel, sometimes I think you're crazier than a bedbug. Why'd you wake me?"

"That kid Mark sent him a message from some fool calling himself, The Discoverer."

So what?"

"The Discoverer is trying to get in touch with me through Dragonfly. Ain't that a hoot?"

"You woke me for that?"

"This clown claims I got an inheritance coming."

"Is he your kin?"

"Not even close. Says he's been hired to find me. Wants to give me a big inheritance. Some long lost relative has died and left me a fortune."

Harry smirked at Hazel, his eyes dancing. "Won't Moon be surprised to find out he's got rich relatives. You two was left on the door step at the Salvation Army, didn't you say?"

"That's what they told me. I was too young to remember any of it. So was Moon." She sat on the corner of the cot and lit a cigarette, inhaled deeply, then blew a cloud of gray smoke into the air. "They named me after the Hazelnut tree that was in bloom by the back door and Moon was named for the full moon that was shinning through it that night." She coughed hard and then picked a piece of tobacco from her lip as she caught her breath. "I picked the name Dutton out of a phone book when I was six and moon was five. Ain't no way we could have any kin folks. Even if there was, how would they know about the name I picked?"

"Some rich cat named Dutton died, and they think you're his relative?"

"Harry, you're dumber than I thought. Can't you see it's a setup? Has to be that guy we took the diamonds from. It's his way of tracking us down."

Harry winced at his blunder, then he grinned sheepishly. "Well, you wanted to hit on him again, didn't' ya? Now's your chance."

"I know that, Harry." She took another drag on the cigarette. "I'm suppose to meet him at the Klondike in Wingate, tonight at nine."

"You still got Dragonfly's disk; sell it to him when he shows up. If he wants it bad enough, he'll fork cash over right then and there."

"Then what? Think he'll just let us walk away? His gang's sure to be hanging around somewhere close by."

Harry studied his fingernails, a shrewd look on his gaunt face. "Don't worry none, I'll be ready for 'em. I'll have several backup plans all figured out by then."

Hazel stared out through the dirty bedroom windowpane at the distant railroad tracks. Then, she crushed her cigarette out on the windowsill. "Somehow, I just knew you would, Harry."

CHAPTER THIRTY-FOUR

The Klondike was almost empty of customers. Mark sat near the back door trying to look inconspicuous while cautiously watching the front entrance. Walpole's chrome-plated pistol tucked in his belt was hidden under his sweatshirt. Betty Ann and Walpole occupied a booth in the other end of the room. Her food hardly touched, Betty Ann whispered, "I'm as jumpy as a frog caught in flypaper."

"Hope Mark's got everyting straight, lady."

"Don't worry about him."

"I don't know. I seen dat guy in action. He's real shrewd, and quick as a rattlesnake." Walpole looked warily over his shoulder. "Dis ain't gonna be no cinch."

Betty Ann reached over and laid a hand on top of his. "When he comes, just be ready to do your part, okay?"

"Dragonfly probably ain't gonna show dis time neither."

Her eyes searching the few patrons still eating, she whispered, "Might be here already."

Suddenly, at the other end of the room, the door beside Mark opened and a clown dressed in a red and white polka dot jump suit with lacy cuffs and a big red Ping-Pong ball stuck on his nose, burst through the door. White face makeup with exaggerated smile lines, big red floppy ears and oversized clown shoes flopping ridiculously on the linoleum floor, while he held a hand painted placards that read, "For a real good time, see the new movie, TICKLE MY FUNNY BONE. Opening soon at the new Monroe Mall Theater."

He laughed in a shrill stage guffaw as he pranced limber legged across the floor and came to a stop at the first occupied booth. Handing out a bubble-gum ball, wrapped in a paper twist, to the two surprised people, he shook the sign in their faces and horse-laughed again. Then he skipped off to the next booth.

All eyes were on him when the door at the other end opened and a woman in stiletto heels, wearing a black sequined dress, and dark teardrop sunglasses slipped into the room. A black net veil partially covered her face as she nudged her plumpish figure into the tight confines of the corner booth.

The clown danced up to Betty Ann and bowed eloquently. He held up a bubble-gum ball just out of her reach. She giggled nervously and reached out for it. Quickly, he took her outstretched hand and kissed her fingertip. Everyone in the room laughed. Then he slapped the bubble-gum ball into her palm and turned and bowed to his delighted audience. They laughed again.

As he pranced away, Betty Ann whispered to Walpole, "Monroe Mall doesn't have a new theater."

"You got dat right."

"Is he the General?"

"He's da same size, dat's for sure!"

"If he thinks a little stage makeup can fool me, he's sadly mistaken. Signal Mark. It's time!"

Suddenly, the door behind Betty Ann opened and there was no mistaking the figure standing in it. Walpole recognized him immediately. As their eyes locked, the General grinned evilly at him. At the same time, at the other end of the room, a man, dressed all in leather, entered. Half hidden at his side under a long leather greatcoat he held a sawed off shotgun.

The clown held up his placard for the gunman to see. Suddenly, the gangster stepped past Mark's table and put his hand in the clown's face and pushed. The surprised buffoon fell backward into a booth and his sign clattered to the floor. "Now that I got your attention, everybody stay in your seats," he said, waving the weapon in the air. "Which one of you momma's boys is Dragonfly?"

Walpole looked over his shoulder at the commotion and Mark slowly released the milkshake glass and brought his hand under the table and rested it in his lap closer to the pistol.

Betty Ann glanced at Walpole. His face was the color of chalk. Putting his hands over his face, he whispered, "I know dat dude. Dat's Snake Rider. Always wears leather and dem snakeskin boots."

Betty Ann whispered, "Why hasn't Mark done something? That snake person's back is to him."

"Da General's in the doorway, behind ya," he whispered, "he's got a gat da size of a cannon, and he's pointing it right at Mark's head. Day got us surrounded!"

The cook, hearing the noise, wandered out of the kitchen. Snake Rider saw the movement out of the corner of his eye. In one swift move, he wheeled and fired. A hole opened up in the cook's chest as he fell backwards into the hanging pots and pans. Pumping another round into the chamber, he swung the weapon back and forth at the terrified people. "Who wants to be next?" he tittered. The woman in the corner booth screamed and fell back into the corner in a dead faint.

General Fitzhammer strolled into the center of the room and looked closely at each person, one by one. He muttered. "Did Dragonfly deliver my message?" Wheeling around, he pointed at the pudgy woman cringing in the corner booth. "Let's start with you," he said, motioning to Snake Rider.

The gunman reached over the table and grabbed the woman and dragged her from behind the booth. Her blond wig fell off, as he dropped her unceremoniously onto a chair in the middle of the room. "Well, if it isn't Hazel, dressed up like queen of the pigs." The General snatched her sunglasses off. "Let's make this quick, you overblown sow. Give me back my diamonds!"

Unapologetically, Hazel glared up at him. "I don't have 'em anymore, sport."

"Oh? Where are they?"

"Wish I knew."

"Give them to me now, before my associate becomes impatient. He's even better with a blade than I am."

"They were stolen, all right?"

"Hold her, while I search this double-dealing bitch." Snake Rider pinned her shoulders back while the General patted her down. Hazel held still for him, an amused smirk on her face.

"Enjoying it, ain't you, sport." She could feel his gloved hand probing between her thighs. "This how you get your jollies?"

He withdrew his hand and shuddered. "So, if you don't have them, possibly your friend Dragonfly has somehow acquired them?"

"Could of been him. He *was* in the neighborhood."

"So, let's ask him."

"I lost track of him, I swear."

"When did you last see him?"

"Been a while; maybe day 'fore yesterday."

The General quickly slapped her hard across the face. "Fool! Don't lie to me."

Blood trickled from the corner of her mouth and she spit it on the floor. "I ain't lying."

"He was in touch with you *today*. That's how you knew to come here." She glared up at him sullenly and spit more blood on the floor. "One more chance, bitch. Where is he?"

She wiped away the blood trickling down her chin with the corner of her perfumed hankie. "Why don't you ask that kid, Mark. He's talked to him more than I have."

"Splendid idea." He motioned to Snake Rider. "Bring that one over here and put him beside this double-dealing sow." Mark sat frozen in his seat, trembling, unable to move.

The gunman jerked Mark to his feet. Escorting him over, he shoved him roughly into the chair beside Hazel. When he landed, the pistol clanked loudly against his belt buckle.

The General grinned. "See what he has there." The gunman patted him down and brought out the pistol and handed it to the General. "Children shouldn't play with firearms," he said, tossing it to the floor. "Now tell me about Dragonfly."

Mark clung to the chair, his face pale. "He's a programmer I met in a chat room. He helped me break a code and stuff like that."

"I didn't ask you for his history. Tell me *where he is!*"

"I don't know. I've never really met him in person."

"While we're at it, I'll take that disk you have."

"I don't have it any more. I gave it to Dragonfly."

"You gave it to Dragonfly? But you have never met him in person?"

"No, no, it's true. I left it with Hazel. She said she'd give it to him."

"What makes you think this fat sow would do that?"

"Because, I talked to Dragonfly on the net the next day. He said he got it and was working on it for me."

"So, we're back to the queen of the pigs again. Somebody's going to tell me where Dragonfly is before this is over." Angrily, he reached out and slapped Mark across his face and he fell backward off the chair onto the floor. "One of you knows where he is!" He turned to Snake Rider. "Watch these two while I talk to the juicy one."

Striding over to Betty Ann, he stared down at Walpole sitting across from her. "How convenient. Even the weasel is here." Walpole ducked his head, and cringed away. Without warning, the general seized Betty Ann's long hair and pulled her face close to his. Inhaling deeply, he cooed, "Delightful fragrance, my dear. Now, what can you tell me about all this?"

She tried to push him away. "I have no idea where your horrible old diamonds are and I've never met anyone named Dragonfly." He jerked her close again. Suddenly, she gave up struggling and said angrily, "You framed my Ted, and he's been running from you and those old Air Force people for almost his whole life." Her words rushing out, she began to sob hysterically. "I hope you find your old diamonds and just leave us all alone. I hate you."

He released her hair, and stood back feigning surprise. "Well, I must say you do have spunk. It sounds as if you might almost be telling the truth."

He turned to Walpole. "What about you, gumshoe? You always wanted to get your hands on my diamonds."

Walpole rolled his eyes and his lip curled. "I ain't got no more use for 'em. Day is bad news, dat's for sure. You couldn't pay me to take 'em now."

"About what I expected from you."

Suddenly, the clown came back to life and pulled out a pistol hidden in his oversized shoe. As he turned it toward Snake Rider, the gangster swung his shotgun like a club, easily knocking it from his hand. It skittered across the floor and came to a stop at the General's feet. He picked it up and sneered, "Don't kill him yet. He may know something."

Walpole blurted out, "He's da one. He's got to be Dragonfly. There ain't no new theater at da Mall!"

The General's cold eyes focused on the clown. "The gum shoe could be right. Wipe that makeup off. Let's see what he looks like under there."

"I ain't Dragonfly," the clown mumbled, as Snake Rider began to remove the grease paint with a napkin. "Don't know nothin' 'bout no computers and such as that."

As the paint came off, the General's eyes opened wider. "So ... the man in the outbuilding! When you tied me up, I told you you'd live to regret it."

"I ain't no Dragonfly."

"Who ever you are, you will not live to trick me again. Where are my diamonds?"

"I ain't got 'em. You was there when I gave my share to Hazel."

"So, she tricked you too?"

"She wouldn't of done that. Somebody else stole 'em."

"Then we're back to Dragonfly. He must be the culprit?"

"If that's what she told you."

"Then we all agree, Dragonfly must have my diamonds!"

"Well, that's what she told you, weren't it?"

"And since you are the logical candidate to be Dragonfly, you have them." Turning to Snake Rider, he said, "Search him. He might have been stupid enough to keep them on his person."

"I done told you, I ain't Dragonfly!"

"Strip him down."

The gangster pulled a long switchblade from his pocket and clicked it open. Quickly thrusting the blade under the neck of Harry's costume, he ripped it down the front.

"Hey! I had to put down a big deposit for this fool getup."

The General pointed his pistol at Harry and grinned. "You won't be taking it back."

"I done told you, I ain't got your fool diamonds." The costume in shreds, Harry stepped delicately out of what was left, and it fell to the floor. His baggy boxer shorts dangled loosely on his skinny body.

There was a shoulder holster with a small caliber pistol strapped to his chest.

The General deftly removed the weapon. "You've got more claws than an ally cat. Any more of these?" Snake Rider placed his shotgun on the floor beside him and searched the costume while the General paced around him, making sure his confederate didn't miss anything.

"You has the wrong 'un, I done toll you that."

"No diamonds, and no disk" the gangster said, "Shall I do him now?"

"Wait. This is your last chance. Where are they?"

"You got the wrong 'un. I don't know."

The General hesitated for a moment. "Let us be gentlemen about this. It is obvious that this has become somewhat of a standoff. Possibly, you are telling the truth. You do not know where the diamonds are and you are not this Dragonfly person that I seek. Let us work together and find Dragonfly and ergo, the diamonds. I will split them with you. Does that not seem fair?"

"I don't know no Dragonfly."

The general's eyes narrowed. "Kill him."

The switchblade clicked open again. Harry stepped out of his floppy clown shoes, and in his bare feet backed away from the man in leather, waiting for the knife blade. It came swiftly at Harry's chest, but somehow it missed. In one quick motion Harry held the knife and it sunk into the gangster's neck.

Snake Rider slumped to the floor and sat, against the wall hopelessly trying to stop his blood from spurting. Harry quickly grabbed the shotgun. At the same time the General stepped behind Hazel. He pulled her to her feet and using her as a shield pointed the pistol at her head. "More claws than an ally cat," he muttered as he cocked the hammer. "If she means anything to you, it would be best to drop that weapon now."

"Go ahead. Kill her, then I'll kill you." Still in a sitting position Snake Rider moaned once and his head slumped to his chest. "Just like this-un on the floor."

"But Dragonfly has our diamonds. I can help you find him."

"Don't need no help. I already knows where Dragonfly is; knowed it all along. You been looking in the wrong place.

"Where should I be looking, then?"

"That's Dragonfly you is holding on to. The disk you're looking for is in her handbag over there in the corner."

The General's eyebrows shot up. "I am constantly amazed at your bumpkin ingenuity!" Quickly dragging Hazel to the booth, using her body as a shield, General Fitzhammer retrieved the disk.

Harry grinned proudly at the General. "Hazel's a damned fine programmer. She's had everybody fooled all along." He took a step closer. "You got what you come for, now let go of her and drop that shootin' iron. I'm getting' tired of all this chitchat."

With his back to Mark, the General dragged Hazel back toward the door. "If she's Dragonfly, *she* must have my diamonds!"

"No they was stolen away, just like we both told ya they was. Don't know who done it."

Mark suddenly saw his chance and reached for the gun on the floor. Pointing it at the General, he cocked the hammer and hesitated. The general heard the sound and turned just as Mark pulled the trigger. The explosion echoed around the room and the old villain slumped to the floor. Harry ran up and kicked the weapon away.

Hazel bent down and felt the general's neck for a pulse. "He's done for, Harry. The kid almost got me too."

"Like the General said, never let young-ins play with fire arms."

"He sure saved my bacon with it, Harry," she said, quickly searching the General's pockets and removed a large roll of bills. Handing it to Harry, she looked back at Betty Ann and shrugged, a smug grin on her face. "For all the aggravation, darlin'."

"Are you sure he's dead?" Betty Ann asked. "He's the proof that Ted is innocent."

Hazel nodded, then noticed Harry trying to find a place to put the roll of bills. "You look ridiculous standing there in your drawers. Take Snake Rider's coat. He won't be needing it. Let's get out of here before the cops come."

EPILOG

The white sandy beach on the tropical island was almost empty of people as the setting sun reflected shades of orange and red in a sparkling azure sea. A suntanned shirtless man with his big stomach hanging over his yellow and blue flowery shorts came out of a grass-roofed cabana. He walked across the warm sand holding two tall frosted tumblers with little pink umbrellas sticking out of them.

The thin woman resting on the hotel blanket at the edge of the water reached up for one of the tall glasses, a satisfied look on her face. "Wonder what they're doing back in Monroe right about now, honey?"

"Most likely, watchin' them big cars motorizin' right along."

Teardrop shaped sunglasses protecting her eyes, she watched seagulls circling over a distant fishing boat. "This is the life, ain't it?"

"Yeah," the big man said. "Y'all want lobster again for supper, Avis?"

"Why not, Moon? We got enough loot to last for two lifetimes."

"Good thing the General stopped me in town that time and ask me if I knowed where Hazel was at."

Avis adjusted the pink umbrella in the tall glass and took a long sip from the barber-pole colored straw. Then she looked up. "Yeah. Lettin' it slip about her and the diamonds and all."

"If I hadn't of told you and you hadn't of remembered what she told you about her hidey place after our wedding party back then, we'd still be back in the states drinkin' Pepsis and livin' on goobers."

"After all that giggle water she drank, Hazel was way too drunk to remember what she'd told me."

"Yeah, well y'all know what the good book says. Do unto others 'for they do unto you, or some such."

"Oh, Moon. You beat all, you know that?"

"Yeah," he snickered. "Y'all ready for another round?"

About the Author

Robert W. Lindsay, who lives in Waxhaw, N.C., attended Elon College, the University of North Carolina, Fred Archer's School of Photography in Los Angeles, and Winonna Advanced School of Photography. He began his career as a commercial and portrait photographer in High Point, NC. After twenty years, he sold Emerywood Studio, to became a textbook representative for Behavioral Research Laboratories in Palo Alto, CA. Later he founded an international Mail Order company, Unfinished Business located in Wingate, NC. Hobbies: Yacht Racing, Ballroom Dancing, Fly Fishing and writing. He has completed to date, two screen plays, many short stories and a book of poems and
The Dragonfly Reprisal is his third full length novel.

His other published mystery novels are:

The Last Chance
The Hidden Room
If You Like These Rhymes You Gotta Be A Redneck

You can find them at: www.lulu.com/boblindsay

This is a work of fiction. Names, characters, places, and incidents either are the product of the author's imagination or are used fictitiously, and any resemblance to actual persons, living or dead, business establishments, events or locales is entirely coincidental.